DATE DUE

SEP 1 1 1997			

Demco, Inc. 38-293

WHO IS VICTORIA?

by Betty K. Erwin

Illustrated by Kathleen Anderson

Little, Brown and Company
Boston   Toronto

Third Printing
T 09/73

Library of Congress Cataloging in Publication Data

Erwin, Betty K
  Who is Victoria?

  SUMMARY: Margaret and her friends spend an unusual
summer after they meet the strange and mysterious
Victoria.
  I. Title.
PZ7.E744Wk   [Fic]   73-7635
ISBN 0-316-24947-5

Published simultaneously in Canada
by Little, Brown & Company (Canada) Limited

PRINTED IN THE UNITED STATES OF AMERICA

46010

WHO IS
VICTORIA?

1

IT WAS early March, with a wild wind and a blue sky, and it was *warm*. For Wisconsin, it was very warm indeed. The snow was gone, the streets were dry, and all over town washings were flapping on the line. It had been warm at morning recess and it was probably warmer now.

It was almost noon. In a minute the bell would ring and the children could run home in the wild March wind for noonday dinner. Now they stirred restlessly in their winter clothes — the long underwear was itching — and began putting away their things.

Margaret scratched at the back of her knee where her underwear seemed thickest and itchiest and tore the last sheet from her tablet. She had to finish her theme this afternoon and now, oh, bother! she was out of paper. If she ran really fast she could get downtown and get another tablet and still get home in time for dinner. That would mean charging the tablet, which she wasn't really supposed to do, and cutting through the backyard of the clinic, where her father would probably see her going the wrong way. Never mind, she had to have paper, and she was going to get this horrible long underwear off, too, no matter what her mother said.

The town Margaret lived in was very small (nine hundred and fifteen people by the 1930 census). Her house was only a block from school, and downtown was only two blocks from school in the opposite direction. The whole trip wouldn't take long, but she ran, along with all the kids who lived on the other side of the tracks, in order to get downtown before the noon train blocked the crossing. She shot into the drugstore, picked up a tablet, and said to the druggist, "Will you charge it, please?"

"Charge it?" asked the druggist. Ordinarily so agreeable, now he gave her only half a smile. "Credit, eh? Well, I guess it's all right. The whole town's buying on credit today. Goodness knows where it will end!"

Well, what's the matter with him? Margaret wondered. A tablet is only five cents. Why, her mother charged dollars' and dollars' worth! She hurried out and almost bumped into Mr. Jolstad. He ran the grocery store across the street. He had white hair and a kind, pink face, and this was the first time she had seen him not smiling.

"You tell your Daddy, Margaret," he said, "not to worry. His credit's always good at my store."

Well, of course our credit's good, she thought. Whatever next?

"Why, thank you," she said, and sped on.

She could hear the train whistle. It hadn't gotten to the crossing yet. She ran faster and beat it, and then she kept running, kitty-corner across the courthouse block, and then across to the Presbyterian church. The train must be late.

Everything is funny today, Margaret thought: the weather, the people, the train. As she hurried along her own block, with the row of poplars on one side and the vacant lot on the other, she could see the sheets blowing in her own backyard and her mother just coming out with another basket. Dad's late, too, she thought, or Mama wouldn't still be hanging out clothes.

Mrs. Evans was wearing house pajamas. This was a new fashion that many of the ladies in town had been following lately. Mrs. Evans had made them herself, taking her turn at the pattern. They were made from a blue and white cotton print, fitted at the top with cap sleeves and a white collar, and cut very full in the legs so the pajamas looked like an old-fashioned dress. Her face was very pink and her hair was curled tighter than usual, because she had been bending over the boiler, stirring all those bubbling clothes and getting steamed herself.

Margaret, whose own hair was dull brown and straight as a string, except when it stuck out from sleeping on it the wrong way, looked at her mother's dark red curls with admiration. She ran up to her mother, panting, and held out the tablet.

"I charged it," she said, "but I'll pay you back out of my own money."

Mrs. Evans picked up a wet sheet and began to shake it out. She looked angry.

"Well, you just can!" she said. "Your father has only eighty-seven cents to his name!"

"What happened?" Margaret asked.

"The bank's closed," Mrs. Evans said. "All the banks are closed, but ours is closed forever."

"You mean, gone broke?" Margaret asked. "Failed? But what's happened to the money, then?" Of course, everyone was used to there not being much money around. First the stock market had fallen apart — that was years ago — and since then the Depression had gotten worse and worse.

"Personally," Mrs. Evans said, savagely shaking out towels and hanging them up with vicious jabs of the clothespins, "I don't think there ever was any money. People just thought there was!" She paused. "Men!" Mrs. Evans said. "Why, I could run the world better than they do with one hand tied behind me. I could run it and do the washing at the same time and do it better than they do!"

"Would you want to run it?" Margaret said.

"Of course not," Mrs. Evans said. "Well, we've got a new President, anyway. We'll see what he can do. Dad's at the hospital. An emergency operation. Let's hope this patient doesn't want to pay us in firewood. I just can't stand to give up the oil burner."

"Here he comes now," Margaret said.

Dr. Evans's car turned into the driveway with its customary flourish. Margaret went into the garage by the back door and met him.

"Hi, Margaret," he said. "Well, the new President is sworn in and we're dead broke. Let's eat dinner."

"Listen, Dad," Margaret said, "what do you think about long underwear in this weather?"

"Well, I've got mine on and it itches," Dr. Evans said, "but the weather could change anytime. You better ask your mother."

"I don't see why," Margaret said. "She wears hardly anything at all herself, just silk stockings right next to her skin, and she makes me dress like I was going moose hunting."

The table was set in the kitchen, as usual. On Sunday or when company came, they ate in the dining room. But when there were just the three of them and the baby in her high chair, eating in the kitchen made serving easy.

"How will it be," Margaret asked, "without any money?"

"Well, we won't starve," Dr. Evans said. "That's one thing about practicing in the country. As long as farmers grow food and farmers get sick, we won't starve. We may have to burn wood and there won't be any trips and your mother will have to make your clothes — "

"She does anyway," Margaret said.

"I don't see that it will make much difference to you," he went on. "We can't complain, living here. Why, there are doctors driving cabs in Chicago. I have a friend who drives a cab all day and works in a free clinic all night, just to keep in practice."

"I am sick and tired of talking about money," Mrs. Evans said, "and from now on this family is not going to do it."

"Mr. Jolstad says your credit's always good, though," Margaret said.

"That man is going to go bankrupt," Dr. Evans said. "He's carrying too many people already."

"I don't want to hear about it," Mrs. Evans said.

"Well, it's a nice day anyway," Margaret said, "and everyone is going to have good smelling sheets tonight. I'll bet President Roosevelt is happy. Do you suppose he had to wear long underwear to the inauguration?"

"If my husband had to sit in a wheelchair outside in

March I would certainly put out long underwear for him," Mrs. Evans said.

"And if I were President of the United States I would make my own decisions," Dr. Evans said.

Margaret finished her ground-cherry sauce and ran upstairs. The windows in all the bedrooms were open to air the house, and the wind hit her from all directions. Oh, it was gay, it was gay! Wild and splendid and full of life! Bare branches swayed outside the window, clouds like huge sails moved rapidly over the brilliant sky. She struggled out of the long underwear but she didn't dare go without her stockings. She untangled her garter belt, got it back on, and then dragged up her long ribbed stockings. They wrinkled at the knees like awnings. Well, hitch them tighter, then! She grabbed a pocketful of marbles, her jacks, and a jump rope.

When she got to school the kids were all out in the playground, playing spring games as rapidly as possible before winter came back. Margaret's three best friends, Polly, Emilie, and Belle, were jumping rope. Polly and Emilie were swinging the rope for Belle. No use waiting for a turn there. Belle could jump forever. Margaret took her own rope and jumped by herself.

> *Fatty Arbuckle sat on a pin,*
> *How many inches did it go in?*
> *One, two, three, four. . . .*

The bell rang. When they got inside the blackboard was full of fractions, and there was nothing to do but sit down and start working them out. The teacher was hearing the other grade give geography reports. They were duller than the fractions.

Since the Depression had started, there were two grades to a room, with one teacher for both grades. It made the rooms rather crowded, but it was interesting, too, because you could always listen to the other class. Of course if you were in the fifth grade and you learned everything the sixth grade did, too, then that didn't leave you much to do when you were in the sixth grade yourself. You could always read the encyclopedia, though.

How strange fractions were, really! They made a sort of sense, of course, but multiplying and dividing seemed backward. In fact Polly, who had a strange mind, had insisted to the teacher that it couldn't be right. To multiply and get an answer that was smaller than you started with, and divide and get one that was bigger — no, Polly said, she just couldn't accept that. The thing about arithmetic is that if you just keep doing it, just keep doing it blindly, the reason for all of it will burst upon you eventually and then you will understand it. It hadn't burst upon Polly yet, though.

The fractions were done, the theme was finished, then came recess, painting, clean up, and finally music. The teacher played the piano and the children sang.

> *Oh, to be a gypsy, and drive a gypsy van,*
> *Up hill and down hill and be a gypsy man.*

Emilie had to go straight home, but Polly, Belle, and Margaret came out in the sunshine together and said, at the same time, "What should we do?"

"I have to take my library book back," Belle said. "Let's go there first."

"I hate to go to the library," Margaret said. "I hate Miss Godfrey. She's so mean and sour and she looks like a witch."

"I don't believe she is a witch, though," Polly said thoughtfully.

"Of course not," Belle said. "Lots of old ladies wear long black dresses and shawls and high-button shoes. She's awfully poor. That's probably all she has to wear."

"I *know* that," Margaret said. "I don't mean her clothes. She acts like she owns all the books and she won't even let you look at any that aren't on your own grade shelf."

"Mama says the committee is too afraid of her to do anything," Polly said, "and the salary is so low they're lucky to have a librarian at all."

"Well, let's go and get it over with," Margaret said. "Maybe there's a book on the fifth-grade shelf I've missed."

The library was in the city hall, and the windows looked out on a green with a bandstand and a great pine tree just outside. The pine tree had lights on it at Christmas time, and the band played in the bandstand in the summer, but just now it was rather bleak. Miss Godfrey was sitting at the desk, looking as sour as usual. Her long full black skirt came right down to the ground. She was small and bony, and she looked as though everything about her had been pinched in narrower than it was intended to be. Margaret sat down at one of the tables and looked longingly at the sixth-grade books. I can certainly read as well as anyone in the sixth grade, she thought, and I can't even touch one of those books. She read through the fifth-grade titles again.

Why, there was a book she hadn't read! She jumped up.

The marbles in her pocket rattled and two of them leaped out and rolled loudly on the floor.

"Margaret," Miss Godfrey said in a piercing whisper, "if you bring marbles into this library again, I will confiscate them."

Margaret picked up the marbles and got the new book, *Maida's Little School.*

She handed the book to Miss Godfrey to be checked out. Mean, horrible witch, she thought, I'll bet you didn't even notice that it was spring today. I'll bet you've never played marbles or jumped rope or even smiled in your whole life.

Polly was pulling at her jacket.

"Come on," she whispered. "Now," Polly said when they were outside, "let's go up the creek and see if there are any pussy willows."

They had a good time following the creek and looking for spring, but they didn't find it.

"After all, this is just the first warm day," Polly said. "Pretty soon there will be pussy willows."

"Look at those black clouds coming up," Belle said. "If you ask me, pretty soon there will be a blizzard. It's getting colder, too."

When Margaret got home there was no one else there. Of course Dad wasn't home yet, and Mama must have taken the baby and gone out. She made two brown-sugar sandwiches and took them into the living room. She sat in the big chair by the radio, all ready to turn on "Jack Armstrong" when it was time, and hung her wet feet over the arm of the chair. She ate her sandwiches and read *Maida's Little School,* listening to the hum of the oil burner and the wind rising outside.

How lucky, Margaret thought, to find a book on the shelf she'd never seen before. Why, she'd looked at that shelf a hundred times! It was funny, strange. Almost as funny as a spring day right in the middle of winter!

2

———◆———

ɪT WAS Saturday morning. Winter had returned. They'd had snow, but most of it had melted and there was a lot of slush around. The temperature was just above freezing, which is one of the most miserable temperatures there is. Everything was wet, the trees and the air and the ground, and the puddles and creeks and rivers had that sullen, cast-iron look that water gets when it's thinking of freezing. The sky was like cast iron too, and the wind went right through your clothes and your skin.

The Evans family ate their breakfast and looked out the window.

"This is the kind of day," Dr. Evans said, "when some woman way out at the end of a dirt road will have a baby, and I will have to crawl out there in the mud."

"Don't complain," Mrs. Evans said; "you love it."

"And this afternoon," he went on, "it's going to freeze. The town will be a sheet of ice. Every old woman in town will go out and fall down. Why don't they stay home when it's icy?"

"They *will* go out today," Mrs. Evans said, "because Hammersted's is having a shoe sale. It's going to be more like a museum, really. He's got out all the old shoes that were stored in the back of the store. They say he has shoes from the eighties, imagine! He's selling them for a nickel a pair. I'm going myself, just to look."

"What I would like," Margaret said, "is a pair of boys' boots, laced-up boots, with a jackknife pocket."

"Well, you can't have them," Mrs. Evans said. "Little girls don't wear boys' boots."

"Then can I wear those old boots of Aunt Eva's that Grandma gave me?"

"When the weather is drier you can. Those aren't wet weather boots. Aunt Eva wore those boots when she was in California and took long hikes in the mountains. I'm sure I don't see why you want to, though. They're too big for you, and those pointed toes look so odd, everyone will laugh at you."

"That won't bother me in the least," Margaret said. It would be nice to wear boots that had walked on the California mountains.

"Can I go over to Polly's?" Margaret asked.

"Polly has housework in the morning," Mrs. Evans said. "Do the dishes and then you can do as you please. There's the baby — " Mrs. Evans hurried out of the room and up the stairs, calling, as she went, "That's all right, Helen, Mama's coming!"

Margaret tore through the dishes, gave the sink a little swipe and swished the broom over the floor. Then coat, cap, scarf, mittens, and overshoes, and she was off through the slush to Polly's house.

When she arrived, Polly said, "Help me make the beds and dust the upstairs and then we can go." Margaret customarily did more work at her friends' houses than she did at her own. They did the beds together and it didn't take long.

"You can go now," Polly's mother said, "but you'll have to come back to stay with Bobby this afternoon. I'm going to Hammersted's shoe sale."

Belle lived just a block from Polly's. "Might as well stop," Polly said.

When the girls asked Belle's mother if Belle could go with them, Mrs. Johnson said, "Well, I don't know; my girls are cleaning. I have too much to do without doing the Saturday cleaning, too, and today I have to make time to get down to Hammersted's. Belle's changing the beds on the sleeping porch. If she's through scrubbing the bathroom floor, she can go."

"That's the biggest bathroom floor in town," Polly said gloomily.

Belle was just finishing the beds, holding the last pillow under her chin and pulling on the case.

"If we divide the floor into thirds and each do one, it won't take long," Belle said. The Johnsons' bathroom had been made out of a bedroom, and a good big bedroom, too. They got through at last.

"Now what?" Margaret said.

"Hammersted's," Belle said.

"You mean after working all morning," Margaret said, "I have to go look at some old shoes?"

"Oh, come on," Polly said.

Hammersted's was jammed with people and full of shoes.

There were bins of old-fashioned high-top shoes, buttoned and laced, some with patent leather bottoms, some with high, curved-in heels. There were adorable high-button shoes for babies, and ladies' pumps with beautiful buckles, all narrow, pointed, and uncomfortable-looking. But a nickel a pair! People were buying.

"It's better than wet feet," the girls kept hearing.

"Grandma wears these anyway," someone said. "I'm going to get her some."

"Look, copper-toed boots! Remember — "

One of the high school teachers was buying shoes to wear with costumes in plays. One woman bought shoes for the buckles. But here and there, farm women, poorly dressed and deadly serious, were going through piles of shoes looking for sizes.

"Do you suppose people are going to wear those?" Polly whispered.

"You heard what they're saying," Belle said. "It's better than wet feet."

"There's Selma's mother," Polly said. "They're on relief, I think. Dad says when people have paid taxes all their lives they have a right to some help in bad times, but I'm glad we don't have to go on relief."

"So am I," Belle said. "Let's not look anymore."

"Let's stop at the grocery and see if they still have that big tarantula in the bottle," Margaret said.

They went around the corner and into the grocery store.

"There's Miss Godfrey buying her potato," Belle said.

"What do you mean, 'her potato'?" Margaret asked. "People don't buy potatoes one at a time. They buy a bushel."

"Haven't you heard that story?" Belle asked. "Ed Paulson

told Ma. She comes in and looks them all over and asks about the potato market, and then she says, 'I'll take that one.' "

"But that's terrible," Polly said. "Is she really that poor?"

"I guess so. If you just had a potato for your supper, I suppose you would pick it pretty carefully."

"She's buying two potatoes and some sausage," Margaret said.

"Well, tomorrow's Sunday," Belle said. "Anyway, it's not polite to stare." They all turned around and looked at the tarantula, which was a large, hairy, and fascinating spider. It had come north on a bunch of bananas and was probably sorry.

"It's almost dinner time," Margaret said. "I better get home. If the baby's up, Mama may want me." This was a lie, sort of, because Mrs. Evans could handle dinner and the baby with ease, but Margaret felt like going home.

"Are you going to church tomorrow night?" Belle asked. "Anyway, we'll see you after Sunday school."

After dinner, Margaret decided she would go see Emilie. Emilie lived on a farm where there was always something interesting happening. It was the last house in town or the first house in the country, and it had a farm attached.

When Margaret got to Emilie's house, Emilie was in the backyard. Margaret could see her distinctly from the sidewalk. When Emilie looked up and saw Margaret, she turned around and ran into the barn and shut the door.

What on earth is the matter with her? Margaret wondered. She ran down the long side yard and banged on the barn door.

"Emilie! What's the matter? Are you mad at me?"

"Of course I'm not mad at you," Emile said from behind the door, "only you caught me, that is — could you go away and come back in five minutes?"

"Go where?"

"Anywhere! I just want to go to the house for a few minutes."

"Oh, all right," Margaret said. She started back toward the sidewalk.

"Never mind," Emilie said, "come on back. You'll have to know sooner or later." The barn door opened and Emilie stepped out.

"Look!" she said.

There was Emilie, looking the way she always did, with her pale blond hair in braids around her head, her eyes as blue as an October sky, and wearing her Saturday skirt and sweater.

"What's the matter?" Margaret asked. Emilie pointed to her feet.

"Oh, your boots! Did you get them at Hammersted's?"

"Mama did," Emilie said. "She said my school shoes are wearing out too fast and I can wear these on Saturdays, to save my others. And after school, too. You know, times are hard for farmers. But aren't they awful? These heels and the pointed toes. I feel exactly like a cow."

"A cow," Margaret said, "why should you feel like a cow?" Both girls looked at the boots. They came halfway up Emilie's legs and were black leather on the shoe part and gray covering the legs.

"Aren't they terrible?" Emilie said again. "I told Mama I'd rather stay in bed than wear them. I said I'd stay in bed all weekend or go barefoot, but she said I can't stay in bed and

I can't go barefoot until summer and they're good sturdy shoes and I have to wear them."

"You know what?" Margaret said. "I have a pair of pointed-toed boots that my aunt used to wear and I wanted to wear them but Mama said everyone would laugh at me. I said I didn't care but then I thought I probably would. But nobody would laugh at two of us. We can wear anything we want to, can't we? It's a free country, isn't it?"

"Would you really want to, though?" Emilie asked.

"I wanted to all along. Can you walk home with me now and we'll get mine?"

"I guess so," Emilie said. "Let's go the back way, through the pasture and the cemetery. Or is it too muddy?"

"I've got my overshoes on. It's beginning to freeze, anyway. Is that dead cow still up in the pasture next to yours?"

"Yes, but we don't need to go near it. Come on."

They walked out of the barnyard, along the lane leading to the nearest pasture. Beyond the pasture rose the steep hills and narrow valleys of Old Hickory. The way was muddy and slippery, but the slush and puddles were beginning to freeze. Some of last year's grass was still there, but the color had been frozen out of it, and now it was like long bleached hair. Over them the sky arched gray. The wind blew cold and drove before it the sullen, tumultuous, rushing clouds.

"Look, someone's coming out of Old Hickory," Emilie said. "It's a girl. See her jumping that little ravine?"

The girl landed on the other side of the eroded ditch and ran down the steep hill.

"Look how fast she's coming. She's going to fall!"

"No, she's not. How funny she looks!"

"Her skirt is so long, that's why. She's going to climb the fence. Who is she? I've never seen her before."

"I don't know," Margaret said. "Who would be up in the fields all alone on a day like this?"

"Let's go meet her."

But by now the girl had slipped between two strands of barbed wire and she was beginning to run again, across the hummocky pasture grass, straight toward them. She made an odd figure. She wore a short, fitted brown jacket, a long full plaid skirt, a little plaid hat to match, and old-fashioned, pointed-toed, laced-up high shoes.

"Look at her boots," Margaret said. "She's been to Hammersted's too."

"And she has long hair," Emilie said. "I thought I was the only girl in town with long hair."

"Hello," called the girl. "Who are you? I've never seen you before."

"I'm Margaret and this is Emilie," Margaret said. "What's your name?"

"Victoria," the girl said. "I'm just running. It seems so nice to run again."

"Have you been sick?" Emilie asked. "If you haven't been running, I mean."

"Sort of," Victoria said. "I have to go now, though. Are you going to church tomorrow evening? To hear the lecture about the Creation?"

"We are going, both of us," Margaret said. "Are you?"

"Yes, I have a special reason for going," Victoria said. "I'll see you then." She gave a little hop, so that her black braids swung from side to side. "I'm going to run all the way home," she said. "See you tomorrow."

"Why, she's running right down our lane," Emilie said, "and she'll have to go through our yard. Who can she be?"

"We'll find out if she comes to church," Margaret said.

The girls turned left and crossed the pasture to the back cemetery fence. They climbed the fence and walked quickly along the aisle between the graves, under the great sighing pine trees.

"Horrible day," Emilie said, "but it won't be long till spring now."

"You know how it is in the summer," Margaret said, "with wild roses all along just outside that fence?"

"And how we're always saying how hot it is?" Emilie said. "Will we ever say it again?"

"Summer always comes, doesn't it? Let's run." They ran all the way to Margaret's house.

"Is that you, Margaret?" Mrs. Evans called as they were coming in the door. "Be quiet, the baby's asleep. If you wake her up, I can't stand it. Hello, Emilie."

"We came to get my boots," Margaret said, "so we can be alike."

"You may start a fad," Mrs. Evans said.

"You said everyone would laugh," Margaret said.

"Not if there are two of you," Mrs. Evans said.

"We saw another girl wearing them," Margaret said, "with long black hair."

"There's a new family in town," Mrs. Evans said. "I don't know their name. The mother of the family has written a song called 'Take the D-I-E out of Depression.' Then it goes on, 'and we will press on with all our might and main.' She's probably their daughter. Be quiet going upstairs and bring the boots down to put on. They clatter."

23

When Margaret came down in her stocking feet carrying the boots, Mrs. Evans said, "Run up to the bakery and get me a loaf of bread, will you?"

Emilie and Margaret marched up Main Street in their high shoes, feeling rather silly.

"Now, let's just be perfectly normal," Margaret said. "If people laugh, just ignore them. Pretend you don't know what they're laughing at."

They met Mrs. Johnson.

"Well, just look at you two!" she said. "Fashion plates from 1915. I had shoes like that when I was, well, I won't tell you how old I was! Don't pay any attention if people laugh! Who knows, maybe they'll copy you. I saw a lot of people buying at Hammersted's."

"We saw a little girl out in the country with shoes like this," Emilie said. "She had long black hair and a pretty long skirt."

"Now who would that be?" Mrs. Johnson said, and she paused. "I know. You remember that family, the parents who were drowned crossing the river when it was in flood? They had a lot of children. I understand they were parceled out here and there. Seems to me they're part Indian. Did she look like an Indian?"

"I don't think so," Margaret said.

"Long black hair and a long skirt sounds Indian to me," Mrs. Johnson said. "Well, I've got to get home. Belle's staying with Georgie. I'll tell her about your new shoes." She hurried off.

"I didn't think that girl looked like an Indian, did you?" Margaret said.

"She looked awfully happy for someone who's living with

a strange family and whose parents have just died," Emilie said. "I think your mother is right. She looks more like the kind to have a mother who would write, 'Take the D-I-E out of Depression.' Anyway, her name is Victoria, and that doesn't sound Indian."

"We'll find out tomorrow," Margaret said. "Do you suppose she'll come sit with us in church?"

The lecture the following evening was held in the Presbyterian church, because it had the best furnace. Since the Depression had started, the churches were short of money, like everyone else. The largest church, the Lutheran, was still prosperous, but the Presbyterian and Methodist churches were sharing a minister, and they used the Methodist church in the summer and the Presbyterian in the winter. The lecturer was a visiting minister, an elderly man who had been a missionary in his youth. His own experiences were interesting to the adults in the congregation, but the children were more fascinated with his lectures on the Bible, because he had pictures of everything. He projected these pictures onto a screen, and there was Goliath, as tall as the Lutheran church, or the walls of Jericho coming down, or John the Baptist's head on a platter.

Sunday evening found Belle, Polly, Emilie, and Margaret in the third pew.

"Will there be dinosaurs, do you suppose?" Belle asked.

"I want to see Eve made out of Adam's rib," Margaret said, "but Dad says it's very unlikely."

"I want to see the waters separate and the firmament become heaven," Emilie said.

"Hush up," Polly said, "he's going to start."

"Victoria's not here," Margaret said.

25

The Reverend Mr. Olson came to the front of the room.

"Let's have the lights dimmed," he said, "and let us read from Genesis I." The lights dimmed. There was a swishing sound in the aisle, and Victoria sat down at the end of the pew.

"Just made it," she whispered.

"And God said, 'Let there be light.' First slide, please," Reverend Olson said.

"Oh, please," Victoria said, right out loud, interrupting everything, "oh, please, Reverend Olson, don't you have a slide *before* that?"

"Before what? Who is that? Lights, please." The lights went on and there was Victoria in her long plaid skirt and short brown jacket. Her little plaid hat tipped to one side of her head and her black braids swung behind her as she stood to address Reverend Olson.

"Don't you have a slide of what the earth was like *before*, you know, when the earth was without form, and void, and darkness was upon the face of the deep?" Victoria's voice shook with eagerness and she clasped her thin hands before her.

"You mean nothingness, chaos?" Reverend Olson said in his deepest voice.

"Oh, yes, I've always wanted to see it!"

"Why, yes, I do," he said. "I do have such a slide, but I don't usually show it. Too many people find it upsetting. But if you wish to see it, would the rest of the congregation be interested?" There was a general affirmative rustle and a gruff "I would" from the back row.

"Dim the lights again. Slide A1, please."

Victoria sat down with a rustle and a sigh.

The slide came on the screen, and the audience gasped. "The earth was without form," read Reverend Olson, "and void, and darkness moved upon the face of the deep."

There, on the screen, was a picture of nothing, a sponge of nothing. There was no light but you could see the nothing anyway. It wasn't wet or dry, it wasn't slimy or greasy, it wasn't any color or shape, and yet it moved aimlessly and you could see things in it, shapes like thistles or mushrooms or great trees that heaved up and changed and fell down and flowed sideways. It was nothing at all, it wasn't real, it had no life, but you kept looking at it, trying to find something familiar in it, like looking at a face with no features, looking vainly at a dish shape and trying to see a nose or eyes. Over this grayed mass of dead sponge something absolutely black passed back and forth.

The congregation stared and stared. It was awful, and yet fascinating. It struck terror into the heart.

Margaret stared until her eyes popped. Why, this is terrible, she thought. I'll dream about this tonight. I wish I'd never seen this; it's going to bother me forever. But I wouldn't have missed it for anything!

She kept staring, trying to bore into that mass. There was a secret in it, there must be. It was the end of the world, wasn't it, and not the beginning. The world had been burned or starved — killed somehow.

"This is chaos," Reverend Olson said. "This is the earth before order, before light and life."

Now the screen was empty.

"Lights, please. Well, young lady, was it what you expected?" Reverend Olson asked. But when the lights went on, Victoria was gone.

After that the screen glowed with light, the water flowed away obediently, the earth grew green, and all the creeping, flying, running creatures came to life and gamboled in the sun. At the very end Adam and Eve could be seen walking hand in hand through the Garden of Eden.

When it was all over everyone went slowly out into the night, saying over and over, so that you heard it from all sides, "Who *was* that girl?" and "How do you suppose they made that slide?" and "Imagine a little girl speaking right up like that! Who *is* she, anyway?"

3

MARGARET woke up in the middle of the night and sat straight up in bed. The telephone was ringing in the next room.

"Hello," Dr. Evans was saying into the phone. He sounded wide awake, too, as he always did. "When did you start? All right, I'm coming. Just tell me again where it is. Which coulee? Oh, that road. Fourth farm from the — all right, hang out a lantern and I'll find it." Margaret listened to him moving around, getting dressed. When she heard his door open she jumped up and ran out into the hall.

"Can I come with you, Dad?" she asked. "I can be ready in a minute."

"Why, Margaret," he said, "what are you doing up? No, I can't take you with me. It's the middle of the night, the roads are terrible, and I may have to get a team. I couldn't possibly take you."

"How can I ever learn to be a doctor if I don't get any practice?" Margaret asked.

"Well, the middle of the night is no time to practice,"

Dr. Evans said. "Anyway, this is a baby case. You'd just be in the way. I'll take you during the day sometime."

Margaret went back to bed. She heard him whistling as he put on his coat and overshoes and presently she heard the car start.

Someday I'll go on calls too, she thought. I'll drive out those lonely roads looking for the light and ford flooded rivers and borrow a team of horses and go across fields as Dad sometimes does.

She lay down and looked at the stars out her window. How does he get dressed so fast? she wondered. A clean white shirt, his tie tied just right, and his hair combed, all in a minute. That's partly why doctors seem so powerful. They have all their clothes on, buttoned up, and sick people are in their nightclothes.

Three more years of grade school, four of high school, and then how many more years does it take to be a doctor? she asked herself.

She thought of her father out on the dark country road. If he got to the top of a hill, she thought, he'd be able to see a lantern a long way.

When she awoke again it was broad daylight. She threw on her clothes and ran downstairs. Helen was in her high chair. She had one of those spoons with the curved handles and she was taking the oatmeal out of her bowl and putting it on the high-chair tray. Dr. Evans was finishing his breakfast. Margaret watched while he ate all the white of his egg first and then put the whole yolk in his mouth at once.

"Why do you eat your egg that way, Dad?" she asked.

"Because I worked my way through medical school washing dishes," he said, "and I resolved never to force anyone to wash a plate with egg on it."

"Don't you try it, Margaret," Mrs. Evans said.

"Will I have to work my way through school, do you think?" Margaret asked.

"I hope not."

"Did you have the baby, Dad?" Margaret asked.

"Yes. The Huberts now have a beautiful baby boy."

"Isn't that wonderful?" Mrs. Evans said. "After all those girls! What did Mr. Hubert say?"

"What do you think? He said, 'I can't pay you today, Doc,' " Dr. Evans said.

"You surely didn't ask him for money," Mrs. Evans said.

"You mean, did I say, 'Here's your baby. Twenty dollars, please.'? Of course not. I know he can't pay. Everybody has money on the brain. It's embarrassing not to be able to pay your bills. Well, I'm going to the hospital. Why are you dawdling, Margaret? It's almost nine."

"It's Easter vacation," Margaret said.

The baby began spooning the cereal from the tray to her mouth. Through a blur of oatmeal she smiled angelically at Dr. Evans and held out her hand.

"No, you don't," he said. "You're not giving me another handful of cold oatmeal." He backed out.

Margaret looked at her baby sister with distaste and began to eat her own breakfast.

"Did you find out who that girl is?" Mrs. Evans asked. "The one who asked for that slide in church?"

"No, no one knows who she is for sure," Margaret said. "Not even Mrs. Johnson, and she always knows everything. Besides, none of us have seen her since that night."

"Seems awfully funny," Mrs. Evans said. "She must go to country school. Well, people are moving around a lot, looking for work."

The phone rang and Margaret went into the hall to answer it.

"It was Mrs. Mosby," she said, coming back. "She said can you be at the church by ten because there's an awful lot to do?"

"What?" Mrs. Evans said. "Is this the day I promised to work on those things for the bazaar? If it is, I'm in trouble because I'm supposed to bake a cake to take to the hospital auxiliary. Oh, dear, it is! Well, I can take Helen with me. She can play in that pen. There's sure to be some other babies there. And you'll have to do the cake, will you? It doesn't have to be a layer cake or anything. Just a sheet cake. Take it over to the hospital by three o'clock, to that room where the ladies fold gauze. The hospital cook makes the coffee. Oh dear, I'll have to rush to get ready and I hope I have something for cold dinner for your father. I won't get home for lunch. Just give him some cold roast beef and cottage cheese and maybe open some cans. Oh, why do I promise these things! They ask you way ahead of time and it seems all right then — "

"Go ahead, Mama," Margaret said. "You'll have a good time and hear all the gossip. I like to bake cakes, anyway."

Margaret whipped through the breakfast dishes while Mrs. Evans got dressed and made the beds.

"Practice your piano lesson first," Mrs. Evans said as she packed the baby in the buggy. "If you do it while the cake is baking you're apt to make it fall. You pound so."

"Don't worry," Margaret said. "I'll handle everything."

But I will *not,* she thought, practice my piano at all. I will just bake this cake and get it over with.

She did everything with extreme care. She separated the eggs and beat the whites until her arms ached. She sifted the flour three times and then sifted it again with the dry ingredients. She creamed the butter and sugar until they were as smooth as custard. She beat and beat the cake and then she folded the egg whites in so gently it took five minutes to do it. Lovely! Light as tide foam, whatever that was.

She shut the cake in the oven and sat down to rest. Everyone would admire her cake and her mother would be proud of her. Amazing, they'd think, that a girl who hoped to be a brilliant physician could also bake a cake. She could probably milk a cow and build a house, too, if necessary!

It would be better to sit quietly in the living room. If she walked around the kitchen, cleaning up the dishes, the cake might fall. She read a book, sitting where she could keep an eye on the grandfather clock in the hall.

At the end of forty minutes she went back into the kitchen and peered into the oven.

Why, what had happened to her beautiful cake? It was flat as a pancake. It *was* a pancake, a big, sticky, chocolate pancake.

What's wrong when a cake doesn't rise? she asked herself. Oh, you're smart, you are, Margaret. You can figure that one out, and so could any moron in the first grade. No baking powder. In fact, now she distinctly remembered not putting it in.

There was no use crying. She washed up the dishes and

began again. It wasn't so much fun this time. There wasn't any more chocolate, so she made a yellow cake. She had just put it into the oven when Dr. Evans came in.

"I've only got ten minutes," he called as he came in the door. "Is your mother gone? Just give me something cold." He looked around at the mess in the kitchen but he didn't say anything. Margaret gave him some beef and cottage cheese. She opened a jar of raspberries and found some cookies and sliced bread.

She felt better when she'd eaten, too, but look at all the dishes! She finished the raspberries, waiting for the cake to be done.

Finally, she opened the oven. What a curious brown color the cake had, like a toasted marshmallow, but at least it had risen. It looked funny, though. But why should it? Her eye wandered over the shelf, where the ingredients still stood out. Salt, vanilla, baking powder — only it wasn't baking powder. That was a yellow box of soda. Well, she thought, lots of things have soda in them. It's just like baking powder; it makes things rise. She put the hot cake on the shelf and cut a little piece of it. It had big holes in it and tasted like — soda. Salty and soapy, like soda.

This time she did cry. Then she threw all the dishes in the sink, scooped the soda cake into the garbage, got another bowl, and started again.

She sifted the dry ingredients first and checked each item again and again. Then she creamed the butter, added the sugar, and creamed again. Now the eggs.

There was only one egg left! She couldn't go and buy eggs now; there wasn't time. She stood there holding the egg.

Just then the back door opened and there stood Victoria, in her plaid skirt and hat, brown jacket, and high shoes. Her braids were untidy and her face was red, doubtless from running in the spring wind.

"Well," she said, "do doctors bake cakes?"

"How did you know I wanted to be a doctor?" Margaret asked.

"I guessed," Victoria said, "and I hope you're better at it than you are at baking."

Margaret had a great desire to throw the egg at Victoria.

Victoria's eyes sparkled and she laughed. "Don't throw it at me," she said. "I didn't mean it."

"I only have one left," Margaret said desperately, "and I need two."

Victoria looked at the egg. She leaned forward and looked very closely.

"It's all right," she said. "Go ahead and break it. Everything's fine."

Margaret stared at Victoria. What did she mean?

"Go ahead," Victoria said again, "I *promise* you, Margaret. It's all right."

Margaret broke the egg into a bowl. It had two yolks!

"You see," Victoria said, "twins."

"Could you see into the egg?" Margaret asked.

"Maybe," Victoria said. "I have to go now."

"Wait — ." But Victoria was gone.

Oh blast, Margaret thought. I forgot to ask her last name again.

She finished the cake and it turned out beautifully. The frosting was just right and swirled on like drifting snow. She took it to the hospital and then she came back and

washed dishes. She was still washing when Mrs. Evans came home.

"What a day," Mrs. Evans said. "Helen! You can't imagine how she behaved." She set Helen on the floor. The baby toddled rapidly across the floor and clutched Margaret fondly about the knees. She smiled roguishly over her shoulder at her mother.

"Look how good she is now," Mrs. Evans said. "My goodness, Margaret, what are you doing? Are you just cleaning up now?"

"Oh, Mama, wait till I tell you!" Margaret said. "I made three cakes. The first one I forgot the baking powder and the second one I put in soda instead of baking powder and the last one turned out just fine, only I had only one egg but it turned out to be double, and Victoria was here and she knew! She said it would be all right. It was just as though she could see into the egg."

"See into the egg?" Mrs. Evans said. "She was just fooling you. I imagine it was an especially big one and she guessed. Still, that was funny, wasn't it? I can see that you've had quite a day, but it'll be a lesson to you to be more careful. But the mess!"

There was a knock at the door, and Polly and Belle came in.

"We came to tell you," Belle said.

"We had to tell you what Victoria did," Polly said.

"Sit down," Mrs. Evans said. "I want to hear this too. Margaret, where's your first cake? Maybe it'll taste like brownies. Leave the dishes for a few minutes. Go on, girls."

"Well," Belle said, "we were sitting on our front steps playing jacks. It was sort of warm and the sun was shining.

Then it clouded up and began to rain a little. We were going to stop playing and then up the walk came Victoria — "

"Running," Polly said. "Emilie says she always runs."

Belle went on. "And she said, 'Keep right on playing. It won't rain here.' She stood by us and held up her hand, and the rain came down hard. It rained in the road and it rained on the sidewalk and it came up and rained just a foot away from our feet, but it never came any closer. It stopped right where Victoria told it to!"

"I even stuck my hand in it," Polly said. "It came down hard, just a foot from us. Isn't that *funny?*"

"Well, I suppose rain has to stop somewhere," Margaret said, "but it is funny. She can see into eggs, too."

"Now, Margaret," Mrs. Evans said.

"Well, listen," said Margaret, and she told them the story.

"What we have to do," Polly said, "is ask her, the instant we see her next time, *who* she is and *where* she lives."

"And *how* she does it," Belle said.

4

EMILIE finished the supper dishes and then she took the slop pail out and dumped it into the trough for the pigs. She watched tolerantly while they gobbled and snorted and put their feet in the trough. Pigs! Whoever named them was a genius, she thought. Then she got a pan of feed and went off to feed the chicks.

Here was no modern brooder house, with little orphan chicks huddling under heat and light. This was an old-fashioned farm. The chicks ran free in a small yard, and when they were lonely, or when the wind blew cold through their yellow down, they crowded together under their nice warm mothers. Emilie sowed the feed over the ground, and hens and chicks went clucking and chirping after it. Then she crouched down and let the little chicks peck from her hand.

She looked very pretty, with the skirt of her blue school dress spread out about her and the yellow baby chicks climbing over her hands. Emilie always looked like a picture from a geography book, her friends thought. In a time when all little girls and most women had short hair, Emilie's was down to her waist. It was very pale blond, like cornsilk, and she wore it in braids around her head. Her nose turned up a little, her cheeks were always pink, and her round blue eyes were as blue as harebells. She looked like a very pretty doll, but she didn't act like it.

The sun was setting. The spring day was ending. Emilie fed the chicks and thought about going away, far away to foreign ports, to Mandalay or Shanghai or Ceylon. She wasn't going to stay here all her life, locked in the Wisconsin hills like the chickens in their yard. She would be a missionary and travel to faraway lands and see the jungles and the temples and the bazaars. She looked into the setting sun and saw it coming down over a ship on the sea. After all, she was Danish, and the Danes had been Vikings. They hadn't always been dairy farmers.

Someone was calling her. Someone was almost screaming her name. Emilie jumped up and went out of the chicken yard. She closed the gate carefully to keep the baby chicks in and turned around. Victoria was coming fast up the side yard in a billow of plaid skirt, calling as she came, like a speeding train.

"I'm here," Emilie yelled.

Panting, red in the face, and wild-eyed, Victoria stopped, grabbed Emilie's arm, and reversed course, dragging Emilie with her, back the way she had come.

"Oh, come quick," she said; "there's this terrible old woman. She's asleep under a tree."

"Where?" Emilie asked.

"Just back there a block or so," Victoria said. "She looks

awful. Ugh! Awful. But someone ought to help her. I think she's sick."

"You should have waked her up and asked where she lived," Emilie said.

"I did," Victoria said, "at least, I tried to. I thought it was too cold for her to sleep there, and she looked so funny. But when I touched her, she opened her eyes and said, 'Go away,' in an awful voice. Oh, I was so frightened!"

"I don't see why you were afraid," Emilie said. They were walking very fast now, back toward town.

"Because — oh, because she was so old, and when she said 'Go away' I had the strangest feeling. I felt as though she really could make me go away. Forever."

"That's just silly," Emilie said firmly. Really, Victoria did look a little crazy, like a frightened calf, rolling her eyes that way. Imagine being afraid of an old woman! People were afraid of the oddest things. Margaret was afraid of birds, and she wouldn't even touch the little chicks, although she didn't mind looking at them. Even Belle, who was as brave as a lion, was afraid to touch frogs.

"There she is," Victoria said. "I was hoping she'd be gone. Under that tree on the corner."

"Where?" Emilie asked. It was still light but the shadows were long on grass and pavement. As they approached the tree she could see what looked like a bundle of old clothes, and then she made out a sitting figure, leaning up against an elm tree with its feet stuck straight out on the grass. Victoria and Emilie stepped off the sidewalk onto the grass and stood looking down at the quiet body of an old woman sitting there.

41

She was wearing high-buttoned black shoes and a full black skirt which lay almost flat on the ground. Her head hung down on the narrow chest, but Emilie knew her. It couldn't be anyone else.

"Why, it's Miss Godfrey!" she cried.

She knelt down beside Miss Godfrey and tried to see into her face. It was an ugly dark red color, and Miss Godfrey was snoring softly. Why, she looks drunk, Emilie thought.

Actually, Emilie had never seen anyone drunk. Alcohol was illegal, of course. There had been Prohibition for thirteen years, since before Emilie was born, but the Women's Christian Temperance Union distributed pamphlets and gave lectures at the school, so she knew all about it. Men who drank liquor staggered about, frequently beating their wives and children before they fell into the gutter in a drunken stupor. It was hard to understand why President Roosevelt wanted to repeal Prohibition. Emilie had fearfully asked her father about this, and to her surprise he had laughed. He said that he personally didn't drink, but that it wasn't as bad as the WCTU people made out. Belle and Margaret had asked their fathers, too, and they had both said it would be nice to have a decent glass of beer again.

And now here was Miss Godfrey, looking exactly like one of the WCTU's horrible examples! But she couldn't be! Even if she knew a bootlegger or had wanted to mix something in a bathtub, she could never have afforded it.

"She can't be drunk," Emilie said. "She must be sick."

"Of course she's sick," Victoria said, "that's what I said, didn't I? Shake her a little. Maybe she'll wake up."

"I don't want to do that," Emilie said. "Shake her yourself, if you want to."

"Oh, no," Victoria said, and she backed away and stood on the sidewalk behind Emilie.

Emilie grasped Miss Godfrey's thin shoulder and shook it gently.

"Miss Godfrey," she said urgently, "wake up. You can't sit here. It will be night in a few minutes. Wake up." She shook Miss Godfrey again and Miss Godfrey's head went back and forth.

Oh, this is awful, Emilie thought. She looked desperately up and down the street. How still it was! There wasn't a soul around. Not a car or a wagon had gone by. All the people in town were in their houses, eating supper, washing dishes, or reading their papers, while she was out here feeling all alone.

"Go get someone," she said to Victoria. "Go knock on a door and get some help."

"I already got someone," Victoria said. "I got you."

"Then you stay here and I'll go," Emilie said.

"No indeed," Victoria said. "If you go, I go."

"Oh, for heaven's sake!" Emilie said. She began patting Miss Godfrey's face. She picked up the bony hands and held them.

"Miss Godfrey, Miss Godfrey, wake up," she said over and over, desperately, wildly, and then despairingly. It seemed a long time, but finally Miss Godfrey stopped snoring. She lifted her head. Her hands moved and her eyes opened, but she didn't seem to see anything.

"Miss Godfrey," Emilie said, "do you hear me?"

"Yes, of course," Miss Godfrey said, "that's my name. Vicky Godfrey. Who is calling Vicky Godfrey?"

"It's me, Emilie," Emilie said. "You went to sleep under the tree. Maybe you felt sick or something."

"I was dizzy," Miss Godfrey said. "I felt so light-headed. I thought perhaps it was that wretched kerosene stove, so I went for a walk to get some air. Who did you say you were?"

"Emilie. You know me, Miss Godfrey. Do you think you can get up now, or should I get some help?"

"Of course I can get up," Miss Godfrey said. "I'm a bit stiff, that's all." She felt around on the grass. "My umbrella," she said.

"It's right here," Emilie said. She put the umbrella in the old lady's hand.

"Victoria and I can help you up and you can lean on us," Emilie said. She turned around. "Come on, Victoria," she said.

But Victoria was gone. Well, of all the strange things to do, Emilie thought, to run away just when I needed her.

Emilie took Miss Godfrey's arm and lifted, and Miss Godfrey dug the umbrella into the ground and heaved, and somehow Miss Godfrey was back on her feet. Emilie put her arm around the old woman's waist.

"You're very kind," Miss Godfrey said, "and I'm sure I'll remember who you are in a minute. I seem to have got muddled. You look familiar. Wasn't there another girl with you?"

"Yes," Emily said, "but she must have run off."

"That's strange," Miss Godfrey said. "I felt as if I were running myself, just a few seconds ago. The mind plays strange tricks, does it not?"

They made an odd pair, going up the street. Miss

Godfrey wasn't much bigger than Emilie, but she was a heavy weight on Emilie's sturdy shoulder. It was only two blocks to Miss Godfrey's rooming house, but it seemed to take forever. It was quite dark by the time they got there. The porch light was on, and the landlady was standing on the porch.

"Oh, thank heaven," the landlady said as they turned into the walk. She ran down the steps and took Miss Godfrey's other arm.

"I've been so worried! You left your door wide open and the stove was on and the window was open — "

"I wanted some air," Miss Godfrey said. "It was that stove. It poisons the air. I'm quite all right now, thanks to this little girl. Her name slips my mind for the moment."

"Why, that's Emilie," the landlady said. "You know Emilie. Now come in and I'll help you to bed. Can you make the stairs?"

"Oh, I have been so worried about her," she said to Emilie. "I can manage now. I'll get her to bed."

Emilie watched Miss Godfrey and the landlady go slowly up the narrow stairs. Then she let herself out and began walking home. It was cold. She walked fast, thinking how worried her mother would be.

When she came shivering into the kitchen her mother was kneeling by the stove.

"Oh, Emilie," she said, "I wondered where you'd got to. See what I have here."

In the space behind the stove, where it was warm, was a box with a new baby lamb in it.

"There were twins," Mrs. Davidsen said. "The other one

is all right but this one is a weakling. Papa thinks we can save it if we keep it warm and feed it by hand."

"Won't the mother mind?" Emilie asked.

"Not when she has the other one." They knelt there and watched the woolly baby, and Emilie told her mother about Miss Godfrey.

"You know, Mama," she said, "at first I thought she was drunk!"

"Oh, Emilie, what do you know about that!" Mrs. Davidsen said. "No, I think it was just what she said. A dizzy spell."

"Did you know her name was Victoria?" Emilie asked. "It's funny. No one would dare call her Vicky, and then she called herself that."

"I suppose that's what she was called years ago, when she was a girl," Mrs. Davidsen said. "She was confused."

"I've never known a Victoria in my entire life," Emilie said, "and now I know two. Don't you think it was queer for Victoria to run away and leave me and not even tell me?"

"Yes, I do," Mrs. Davidsen said. She reached for the bottle of warm milk and held it for the little lamb. "But some people *are* queer, you know, Emilie. Not everyone is responsible."

I was responsible, Emilie thought. On the other hand, if I'd been as frightened as Victoria was, I might not have been responsible either, so maybe it's nothing to be proud of.

5

A FEW DAYS before Decoration Day, Mrs. Evans went to the city to buy cloth for summer dresses. She also got Margaret two new books and a little suede marble bag and twenty-five new marbles, the beautiful kind, not to play with but to look into. They were like crystal balls or tiny worlds or pieces of sky, and Margaret loved them. The day before Memorial Day she put them in her bag and put the bag in her pocket and went to see Polly. It was the last day of school, so the children had been let out at noon. On the way to Polly's, Margaret stopped at the library to return her mother's library book, and Miss Godfrey took her marbles.

It was a simple, horrid incident. Margaret handed the book to Miss Godfrey and then she knelt down to tie her shoe. Her pocket tipped sideways and the bag must have come open, because the marbles slipped out and bounced and rolled about the wooden floor. They sounded like bowling balls.

"Margaret," Miss Godfrey said, "gather those marbles together and give them to me."

Margaret was still kneeling on one knee. She looked up at Miss Godfrey, up the stiff folds of black skirt and narrow black chest to the tight pinched-in face. Miss Godfrey looked as stiff as the chair she sat on.

Margaret picked up the marbles and gave them to Miss Godfrey.

"When can I have them back?" she asked.

"One week from today," Miss Godfrey said, and she put them in her purse.

Margaret turned and walked out of the library. Why did I do it? she wondered. Why did I let her bamboozle me like that? I didn't need to give them to her. She can't make me do anything. The old witch must have hypnotized me!

Polly was coming along the walk.

"Hi," she said, "I called your house and your mother said you'd be here. What's the matter? You look funny."

"I am funny," Margaret said, "I'm crazy. Miss Godfrey took my marbles."

"Your new ones?"

"Yes."

"Never mind, she can't keep them," Polly said. "Don't get mad. It doesn't do any good. You know, I was just thinking. School's out. It's a free country. We can do anything we want. Anything at all. We can run and scream and roll down hills and go anywhere. It's almost hard to decide what to do first."

"What I wanted to do," Margaret said, "before I got so mad at Miss Godfrey, was go down to the dam and look for violets and then go up on the hill and look for may-

flowers, and maybe, well, it sounds kind of silly, look for Victoria."

"I keep wondering about her, too," Polly said. "But you can't tell where to look, can you? She could be anywhere."

"Well, then let's go anywhere," Margaret said.

Spring had come overnight, as usual, and now it was almost summer. For weeks they'd watched the progression from icicles to slush to mud, and now all of a sudden the trees were rounded with new leaves, the apple blossoms were out, the hedges were in bloom, the grass was green and needed mowing, and the sun was hot. Margaret and Polly wore summer dresses left over from last year, faded with much washing and rather short. They felt light and free, like shorn sheep.

They went down to the dam and crossed the footbridge over the thundering water. On the other side they found carpets of purple violets and, farther on, a little field of yellow violets. They didn't pick any; they knew the wild flowers would wilt before they got home. Then they went back into town and crossed the bridge and climbed Town Hill. From the top they could see a long way, and they looked for a flash of plaid skirt, a little girl running, but they couldn't see her.

"She probably has to stay home with her little brother or something," Polly said.

"I suppose so," Margaret said, "but she doesn't seem like the kind of person to stay home and wash dishes or things like that." They found some mayflowers and some Johnny-jump-ups.

"In books," Margaret said, "these are out on the first of May."

"But in real life there's apt to be snow on May Day," Polly said.

They came back through town and took the long walk to Emilie's. At Emilie's there were baby chicks and yellow ducklings and a new calf, and Emilie and her mother were baking cookies.

"We're looking for Victoria," Polly told Emilie.

"We haven't seen her for weeks," Emilie said. "I think she's moved away."

By now the sun was going down, and there was still no sign of Victoria.

When Margaret got home, the family was already having supper: cold meat and cheese, fried potatoes, new bread, pickles, and leftover pie. Margaret was too hungry to talk, but after her first round of everything she said:

"Miss Godfrey took my marbles today."

"What, your new ones?" Mrs. Evans said. "What were you doing?"

"Miss Godfrey!" Dr. Evans said. "Is she working? I told her to stay in bed."

"Well, she isn't," Margaret said.

"Been having dizzy spells. In fact, she blacks out. Now don't repeat that, Margaret!"

"Of course not," Margaret said, "I never tell anything. But don't people have to do what you say when they're sick?"

"Of course not," Dr. Evans said. "What do you think I am? A policeman? She asked my advice. She's old, her blood pressure would break the machine, and she's running a little sugar, so I said stay in bed. But if she doesn't want to, that's her business."

53

"Well, if you'd insisted, maybe she wouldn't have made all this trouble," said Margaret.

"I don't run people's lives, thank heaven," Dr. Evans said.

"When you're through, Margaret," said her mother, "go up and try on your white dress. You'll have to wear it for the parade tomorrow. I've let it down to the last quarter inch, but if it's still too short I suppose I can make a ruffle."

"I forgot about the parade," Margaret said. "Are you going to march, Dad?"

"I can't get into my old army uniform anymore," Dr. Evans said, "but I may walk with the Legionnaires."

Margaret tried on her white dress, which looked ridiculous with her scruffy school shoes, and was certainly rather short. Then she went over to Polly's and played anti-i-over until it got too dark and then tickety-can with Belle and Polly until they had to go in. She walked slowly home, taking the long way around.

A bridal-wreath hedge ran the whole length of the Evanses' lot. Heavy and solid white with blossom, it was like a row of ghosts in the moonlight. As Margaret came the last little way, Victoria stepped out from behind the hedge.

"Hi," she said, "where have you been? I've looked for you everywhere all day."

"We were looking for you," Margaret said.

"Isn't that silly? I have to go now, though. Are you going to march in the parade tomorrow?"

"Sure."

"I wish I could," Victoria said. "Maybe I'll come and hang around."

"I'll bet our teacher would let you march with us," Margaret said.

"I'll see," Victoria said, "but now I have to go. Oh dear, I — I — "

"What's the matter?" Margaret said. She peered at Victoria in the dark, trying to see what was the matter.

"I can't remember where to go. I'm lost." She did indeed look lost. She looked small and miserable and lost.

"You're fooling, aren't you?" Margaret asked. "Aren't you going home?"

"That's just it. Where is my home?"

"If you really don't know," Margaret said uneasily, "you better come in the house and we'll call your mother."

"No, it's no good doing that," Victoria said. "I'll just run around and pretty soon I'll remember. And I'll come to the parade if I can."

"Wait," Margaret said. But Victoria was gone again.

"Better go straight to bed," Mrs. Evans said when Margaret came in the house. "I'm going myself. Dad had to go to the hospital. A broken arm, I think. And Miss Godfrey had a stroke, poor old thing."

"A stroke!" Margaret said. "Now when will I get my marbles?"

"Margaret! What a thing to think of! Aren't you sorry?"

"Well, I suppose I am, in a way," Margaret said uncomfortably. "I wouldn't want anyone to be that sick, not even an old bat like that. Maybe Dad can look in her purse."

"Dad cannot look in her purse," Mrs. Evans said. "You'll just have to hope she gets better."

"Oh, I do, Mama," Margaret said. She did, too. It wasn't nice to think of Miss Godfrey paralyzed.

"I saw Victoria," she said as she started upstairs, "and she said she might come march with us tomorrow."

"Oh, I hope so," Mrs. Evans said, "I've never seen her and I've heard so much about her. I'd like to see her for myself."

As it happened, Mrs. Evans had her wish. The very next day, she saw Victoria, and so did everyone else. The whole town got a really good look.

The parade assembled at the school. Margaret was a little late and she expected the ranks to be already forming when she hurried into the schoolyard. But the World War veterans were standing around the front yard, and the school children were still inside the building. She stopped and stared curiously at the men in their uniforms. They were all friends and neighbors, as familiar to her as people in her own grade, but they looked different — trim, remote, and younger than usual in their high-buttoned khaki jackets and knickers, with puttees wound like bandages above their boots. There was a big black car at the curb with four Civil War veterans in it. They wore wide-brimmed hats and two of them had beards. It had been a long time since they had marched to war, and now they couldn't even walk in the parade.

When she went inside the school, it seemed strange to her, too. Already it had a scrubbed, empty look, as though it would do quite well without children for the summer, and the children in their white clothes looked out of place among the cleaned-out desks and washed blackboards. Margaret went into the fifth- and sixth-grade room and found Belle, Polly, and Emilie.

"Isn't it late?" she asked. "Why don't they start?" They all looked automatically at the clock, which had stopped for the summer.

"Haven't you heard?" Belle said. "Gertrude Nelson has

the measles. Mr. Parr is looking for someone to take her place as drum major."

"And naturally no one wants to have to lead the parade without any practice," Emilie said.

"I would like to," Polly said, "if I were in high school."

They went out into the hall and saw the band director hurrying by, carrying a drum major's hat and jacket. He was talking to himself like the White Rabbit.

"That's her uniform," Belle said. "Mrs. Nelson told Ma. They thought Gertrude just had a cold but then she came out in spots last night and this morning she's a hideous sight. So Mrs. Nelson brought the uniform so someone else could wear it."

"There's Victoria," Emilie said. "I didn't expect her, did you? Wave to her."

"She said she'd like to march with us," Margaret said, "and I said the teacher would probably let her, but I forgot to tell her to wear white."

"She always wears that plaid skirt," Polly said. "It's probably the only one she has."

"Am I late?" Victoria asked, coming up to them.

"They're trying to find someone to lead the parade," Emilie said. "The drum major is sick."

"Oh!" Victoria exclaimed, turning quite pale. "Oh, my goodness, I would *love* to lead a parade. All my life I've wanted to lead a parade. Could I ask someone if I could do it?"

"I think they want a high school girl," Belle said hesitantly, "because you'd have to be tall. They want someone more than ten years old."

"Ten years old!" Victoria repeated.

"Well, eleven, or maybe twelve," Belle said. "*I* don't know how old you are."

"No, you don't, and no one else does, either. I shall stand very straight and tall and say I'm fourteen. Who should I ask?"

"That tall man over there carrying the hat, with the baton under his arm," Polly said.

They watched as Victoria set off down the hall after Mr. Parr.

"My goodness," Polly said, "imagine doing that! I would never dare."

"Well, she stood right up in church and asked for that slide," Emilie said. "She has a lot of courage."

"She looks taller," Belle said. "I guess I never noticed how tall she was."

They began to walk down the hall after Victoria. They saw Mr. Parr pointing at Victoria's plaid skirt and old-fashioned boots and then Victoria talked some more. She folded up her braids and held them on the back of her head.

"She's telling him she can pin up her hair," Margaret said.

"It isn't as if she had to twirl the baton or anything," Polly said. "They don't do that for Decoration Day because it's a sad occasion."

They saw Mr. Parr demonstrating. First the whistle, then four beats, then the baton is raised, then four more beats, and then down with the baton when the music starts. He marched down the hall, lifting his feet high and swinging the baton. Victoria marched beside him and imitated everything he did.

"Look at that," Belle said. "He's going to let her do it."

Mr. Parr beckoned to the third-grade teacher, who came over and took Victoria off to the teachers' room. In two minutes Victoria was back wearing the high hat on top of her pinned-up braids. She still wore her plaid skirt and boots, but the uniform jacket, which was short and white and buttoned with two rows of brass buttons, gave her an entirely different look.

Mr. Parr was nodding approvingly.

"Rather a good effect," he said. "Almost Scotch."

Victoria swung her baton and grinned at the girls.

"Isn't it wonderful?" she said.

They lined up in the street, the band, the color guard with streaming flags, the veterans with guns on their shoulders, the high school students, the grade school students with kindergarteners last, and then the big black car with the top down and the four smiling Civil War veterans.

Victoria blew her whistle. She raised her baton, and then down it came and the music and the marching feet moved together. As the parade turned the corner, from their lowly place in the ranks Margaret, Polly, Belle, and Emilie could see Victoria, high-stepping in her old-fashioned boots, her plaid skirt swinging with a martial air, like a Highlander lady going into battle. They would never have had the nerve. They envied her a little, but they were proud of her, too.

The parade marched up to the end of Main Street. The sidewalks were lined with people, and ladies sat on their front porches and watched. Margaret saw her mother, sitting on the Hagers' front porch. She was hanging onto the back of Helen's dress (the baby, as usual, was trying to break free) and staring at Victoria.

The paraders turned right at the end of Main Street and

marched the two short blocks to the cemetery gates. The school children, who were not allowed inside, split ranks and moved to the side of the road, where they sat on the grass until the ceremony was over. With muffled drums and lowered flags the veterans passed into the cemetery and the black car rolled slowly in behind them.

Victoria came over to sit on the grass with Emilie, Polly, Belle, and Margaret.

"Well, how did it feel?" Polly asked.

"Wonderful," Victoria said, "even better than I expected. I'd always wanted to do it and now I have." She lay back on the soft new grass and stretched.

"Have you got a lot of other things you want to do?" Emilie asked.

"Oh yes, quite a few," said Victoria. "I may not get them all done, but I just grab when I get a chance. There isn't much time, at least not enough to do everything I want to do."

"There's lots of time," Belle said. "We're just kids."

From somewhere in the cemetery the bugler blew taps. The mourning notes came to them through the sunny air and they looked at each other, suddenly a little scared. Not enough time?

6

BELLE put the last dish in the dish drainer. Then she got the kettle of boiling water from the stove and poured it carefully over the dishes. From the dining room came the sound of the sewing machine. Mrs. Johnson had set up her portable machine on the dining table and was rapidly turning out summer clothes for her three daughters, all of whom were outgrowing their old ones at a phenomenal rate. Although to Belle the machine seemed to run almost nonstop, Mrs. Johnson was able to keep an eye on everyone passing the window, and she commented vigorously as she sewed.

"There goes Cathleen," Mrs. Johnson said, "and she has a new bicycle. A new bicycle and a new dress. Her Pa's business is doing very well, I've heard. There goes Reverend Batchelder. Now, what would he be doing down this way? Who's sick?"

Belle smiled at her mother's interest in the neighbors. All the girls teased their mothers for gossiping so much, but really, it was natural. She gossiped herself, and so did her friends. So many things happened in town, and there were always strange stories, secrets, and rumors. You couldn't help being interested.

"There goes Martha," Mrs. Johnson said, raising her voice as the machine went into a violent crescendo on a long seam. "What do you bet she's going over to Delores' house and leaving Polly to take care of Bobby. If Polly's going to have Bobby anyway, you won't mind keeping an eye on Georgie, will you, Belle? I've got to do my shopping, and I need buttons, and then I'm going to coffee at Wilsons'."

"Oh, Ma," Belle protested. She just said this out of habit. She always took care of George, and she really didn't mind.

"It isn't as though he was a baby," Mrs. Johnson said. "You don't have to watch him all the time. Just keep a little track of him, is all. I don't even know where he is right now. Look around for him, will you, Belle?"

"Yes, Ma," Belle said. She took off her apron, went out the kitchen door, and looked up and down the street. Then she walked around the corner and looked up that street.

George was running up the sidewalk, coming fast, as though he were being chased. When he saw Belle he ran faster. Finally he ran right into her. It could have knocked her over but she was braced for him. This was what George always did when he was really upset. He grabbed Belle and held on to her.

"What's the matter?" she asked. She put her arms around his small, sturdy body. He wasn't crying.

"Oh, I just saw something," he said. "Belle, I just saw something scary."

"What was it?"

"It was a face. I *think* it was a face." He looked up at her.

"There's someone up there. Right up there, looking out, with hair all over his face."

"Was it in the loft over the blacksmith's shop?" she asked.

"Yes, have you seen it too?" he asked.

Belle smiled at George and hugged him. She remembered the first time she'd seen that face. It still frightened her. Every time she went past the blacksmith's she looked for it, and, either way, whether she saw it or she didn't, she was a little bit frightened.

"I was watching them shoe a horse," George explained, "and then I looked up at the loft window and there it was. Who is it, Belle? Is someone shut up in there?"

"It's nothing to be afraid of," Belle said. "It's a dog, that's all."

"It isn't a dog," he said. "It doesn't look like a dog. It's an old man with his hair all grown out. Nobody would keep a dog in a loft. Not unless — is it a mad dog?" His voice was shaking with excitement.

Belle shook her head. There were a lot of interesting stories about what was up in the blacksmith's loft. Some people said it was a dog that was so vicious it had to be shut up. A lot of the kids didn't think it was a dog at all, but they didn't know what else it could be. A monster, maybe.

"Ma says it's just an old dog that ought to be put away," Belle said, "only the blacksmith is too fond of him to do it. She says the dog is partly blind and a nuisance, and he sleeps all the time, so they leave him up there."

"If he's a dog," George said, "why doesn't he look like a dog?"

"Because he's an English sheep dog," Belle said, "and they have long hair over their eyes."

"I don't believe it," George said. "I'm going back and look again."

"Go ahead," Belle said, "just be careful of the horses."

She went back into the house.

"I found Georgie," she told her mother. "He was all worried about that dog in the loft over the blacksmith shop."

"I've never known whether that dog was mean or not," Mrs. Johnson said. "They take him out at night sometimes, I guess. Seems to me they take awfully good care not to let anyone get a good look at him."

"I thought you said he was really old," Belle said.

"Well, he is," Mrs. Johnson said. "Anyway, it makes a mystery, doesn't it? A little mystery is good for kids."

Presently Mrs. Johnson went upstairs and Belle went up the street to find George. He was standing on the sidewalk opposite the blacksmith's, looking up at the empty loft window. The forge was going, the sparks were flying, but George wasn't looking at the blacksmith or at the horse being shod. He was staring over them, up at the window.

"Hi," Belle said. "Seen anything?"

"I've been here all this time," George said, "and I haven't seen a thing. But Pete Nicholson said it's a terrible dog that bites anyone who comes near it and Jim Paulsen said it's not a dog at all! He said it's a raving maniac that they keep chained up there. What's a raving maniac?"

"A crazy person," Belle said, "and that's just silly. Come on, you don't want to stand there all day."

"Just another minute," he said. "I just want to see it once more."

"What *is* it? What are you looking at?" someone asked.

It was Victoria. She had appeared from nowhere as usual, and now she stood beside them.

"We're waiting for the hairy face," George said. "Something's up there, in the loft over the shop."

"It's probably asleep," Belle said. "Let's come back some other time." But just then, poking out of the shadows, came a featureless, hairy face, looking (but it had no eyes!) out of the loft window.

"But what *is* it?" Victoria asked.

"It's just a dog," Belle said, "an old sheep dog. I've been explaining this all morning."

"Or else a raving maniac or a werewolf," George said.

"Can't it get out?" Victoria asked.

"No, that's where they keep it."

"Well, that's terrible," Victoria said. "I'm going to give that blacksmith a piece of my mind."

"It's gone again," George said, "and I didn't get a really good look."

"That's why it's a mystery," Belle said, "because no one ever gets a very good look. I'm getting tired of this, aren't you, George?"

"I'm going over there," Victoria said.

"But he's busy," Belle said; "the blacksmith is busy. He won't want you bothering him."

"I don't care," Victoria said. She strode across the road in her high-heeled boots, looking odder than ever. Belle and George followed her.

"I want to know — " they heard her say.

"Hey, watch out, get out of there!" A farmer, backing up a huge horse, had yelled at her. Victoria leaped nimbly out of the way of the horse and approached the blacksmith.

"Good morning," she said. She stood very straight beside him with her hands behind her back and her little plaid hat tilted over one eye. She looked like a picture from a Louisa May Alcott book.

"Hi," the blacksmith said. "I've seen you in church."

"I would like to know what you have shut up in your loft," Victoria said.

"I don't see that that's any of your business," the blacksmith said.

"No," Victoria said agreeably, "it isn't, but I want to know anyway."

"Why?" the blacksmith asked.

"Because it's cruel to keep anything shut up," Victoria said.

"It is not cruel," the blacksmith said angrily. "It would be cruel to put him away and I won't do it. He's safe up there, and he just sleeps, mostly. I take him out at night. Now, run along, I'm busy."

"But you haven't told me what it is," Victoria said.

"All right," the blacksmith said, "if you're so nosy, go up and see."

"All right, I will," Victoria said.

"No, don't," Belle said. "It might bite you."

"Would it bite me?" Victoria asked.

The blacksmith shrugged. "Go up and see," he said again. Then he turned his back on Victoria and picked up his hammer. The farmer laughed.

"Come on, Victoria," Belle said, "we don't belong here."

"No, I'm going up," Victoria said. She walked into the shop and looked around for the ladder.

George clutched Belle's hand. "What if it really goes after her?" he said. "What will we do?"

"It's probably tied up," Belle said.

Victoria began to climb the ladder. Belle stood there, undecided. She didn't want to go up there herself, but it seemed cowardly to let Victoria go alone. Slowly, she started toward the shop.

"You stay here," the blacksmith said to her. "She wanted to find out. Let her. Curiosity killed the cat."

"And satisfaction brought it back," Belle said. "You wouldn't have let her go up there if she was going to get hurt."

She wasn't as sure as she sounded. Standing in the sunlight and looking beyond the glowing forge into the dark shop, it was hard to see much, but by now Victoria must be all the way up the ladder. There was a dead silence while they waited for her. Even the horse was quiet, and the blacksmith and the farmer stood there like blocks of wood. It seemed a long time before the high-topped boots appeared on the ladder.

Victoria came slowly down and walked out of the shop to where they all stood waiting.

"He's asleep," she said to the blacksmith.

"I told you so," he said.

"Does he dream?" she asked.

"Sure, he probably dreams he's young again," he said.

Victoria smiled enchantingly at the blacksmith. Her thin face lit like a candle.

"Then in his dreams, he's free," she said. Then she turned to Belle and George. "Come on, Belle," she said, "we're in the way here."

As though it was my idea to be in the way, Belle thought angrily.

"What is it?" George asked. "What did it look like? Was it a dog?"

They walked slowly back toward Belle's house.

"It could have been," Victoria said doubtfully. "It's huge. It could be a bear. It just looked like a big pile of fur."

"Were you frightened?" George asked.

"Yes," Victoria said, "but I had to know."

"I think you were awfully brave," Belle said.

"Couldn't you tell for sure what it was," George asked, "a bear or a dog?"

"Well, if it's a bear," Victoria said, "it will dream it's a cub, and if it's a dog, it will dream it's a puppy. That's the only way to tell."

"That's dumb, Victoria," Belle said. "How can we tell what he's dreaming?"

"We'd have to get into his dream," George said, "and you can only get into your own dreams."

"Well, I should hope so," Belle said.

"I feel a lot better," Victoria said. "I'd been wondering about that loft for a long time."

"I thought you'd never seen the face looking out before," Belle said.

"I hadn't, but I'd heard about it," Victoria said. "It was one of the things that I'd intended to find out about."

"One of the things you've always wanted to do?" Belle asked.

"Well, sort of," Victoria said.

"Coming with me up to Polly's?" Belle asked. She never

could tell whether Victoria wanted to stay around or not. She seemed to come and go so strangely.

"There are Indians in town selling baskets," Victoria said, "and I've always wanted to talk to one. And I have to go pretty soon, anyway."

"Where?" George asked. "Where do you go? We'd like to know, wouldn't we, Belle?"

"That's my business," Victoria said. "I'm just going, that's all. I'm going to find an Indian squaw and ask her some questions and then I'll be off."

"You're always so interested in other people's business," Belle said, "but you don't tell anything about yourself."

"I know it," Victoria said, "but I can't help it." And she went off up the street, walking faster as she went and breaking into a run at the corner.

Belle and George went on over to Polly's. Polly called Bobby and sent him off to play with George.

"Go and play," she said. "Shoo! Go somewhere but not too far." The two little boys trotted off together.

"It always seems funny that we're the same age and that we have little brothers the same age," Polly said.

"It works out so well, too," Belle agreed. Then they sat on the porch steps and Belle told Polly about having just seen Victoria.

"Let's walk around and see if we can see her again," Polly said. They walked slowly up to Main Street and then strolled along it.

"There's one of the squaws selling baskets," Belle said. Across the street was an Indian woman with an enormous bundle slung over one shoulder. She wore a long, full polka-dot skirt and a blue blouse, and her long black hair was pulled back in a bun. She was an elderly woman. Her face was dark and wrinkled and her eyes were like prunes.

Belle and Polly stared curiously. They knew it wasn't nice to stare, but they didn't see Indians very often. In the summer the Indians lived in huts made out of bent branches and canvas on the reservation, and the women came into all the little towns to sell baskets.

"Victoria would probably go right up to her and ask her how to weave baskets," Belle said enviously.

There was a puppy trotting behind the Indian woman. Roly-poly, long-haired, falling over its oversized feet, sniffing everything available, it looked like a teddy bear or a wind-up toy.

"What an adorable puppy," Polly said, "do you suppose it's hers?"

"I wouldn't think she'd bring him into town," Belle said doubtfully, "but I don't know who else here has a puppy like that."

When the Indian woman turned and went up the walk to a house, the puppy left her and came cantering across the street to Polly and Belle. Shaking all over with friendliness, wagging fore and aft and standing on their feet, he reared up and greeted them each in turn.

"Isn't he sweet," Polly said. "Wouldn't Bobby and Georgie love him!"

"We better take him over and see if he belongs to the squaw," Belle said.

The Indian woman was standing on the Mosbys' porch. She looked at the girls and the puppy and simply shook her head.

"She doesn't seem to think much of us," Polly said as they turned back toward the street.

"Let's go home and find the boys," Belle said, "and if the puppy follows us, why, he follows us — we can't help it — and then they can play with him together."

So they walked home with the puppy running in circles around them and making darts at their feet. All that long summer day the little boys played with the dog while Polly and Belle sat around and talked, made lemonade, and played jacks.

The sun was halfway down the sky and the shadows were long on the grass when Victoria came back again. She stood and watched the puppy rolling on the lawn.

"So it was a dog after all," she said to Belle.

"*What* was a dog?" Belle said.

George got up from the grass.

"This is a real dog, Victoria," he said. "It's not in the old dog's dream."

"Are you sure?" Victoria asked.

"Of course I'm sure," George said, "and I'm going to keep him."

"Oh, George," Belle said, "you mustn't count on that. He probably belongs to someone."

"And anyway he's gone," Bobby said.

They looked around, but the puppy had disappeared.

"He can't be gone," George said. "He was right here."

"He probably ran home to get his supper," Belle said.

"But he'll be back, won't he?" George asked.

"Maybe," Belle said.

"You think he won't," George said. The he turned to Victoria. "But he was real. He was as real as you are." He took hold of Victoria's arm and shook it. "Wasn't he?" he asked her. "Wasn't he real?"

"Of course he was real," Belle said. "Don't tease him, Victoria."

"I'm not teasing him," Victoria said. "Maybe I'm wrong. I think I know something and then I'm not sure. I say silly things sometimes. Maybe you're right, Georgie." Victoria rubbed her forehead, as though she had a headache. She looked pale and small.

"Oh, what difference does it make?" she said, and walked off.

7

IT WAS a hot, lazy day in June. The earth, prodded by the sun, was working overtime, and everything was growing fast. The corn in the fields was rising steadily, and the rows of vegetables behind the house were growing thicker. The wild roses along the cemetery fence were out, and down by the tracks the snakeflowers bloomed.

Margaret sat on the front steps of her own house. She felt too lazy to go find someone to play with and too lazy to play anything, anyway.

Dr. Evans's car came up the street and stopped in front of the house.

"Hey, Margaret," he called, "I have to make some country calls. Do you want to come with me?"

Margaret got up and ran to the car. She loved to go on calls. Actually, if her father was willing to take her it meant that the people weren't sick in any interesting ways, not cut up or mangled by threshing machines, and having no broken bones or new babies. Probably just old people or little kids with fevers. Even then she sometimes had to stay in the car.

Margaret understood that people didn't want little girls snooping around when they were sick, but she couldn't help being interested.

Dr. Evans ran his window all the way down so that the hot wind rolled over them, and then he lit a cigar. Margaret hastily rolled her window all the way down and turned her head into the wind. Cigar smoke made her a little carsick.

"It'll be cooler in the country," Dr. Evans said.

It was, too. They took the main road for a couple of miles and then turned onto a side road not much wider than the car. The deep ditches at the sides were full of white clover and wild asparagus, and beyond them the fields and pastures rolled in endless hills, broken occasionally by farm buildings and patches of woods.

Presently they turned into a long, narrow lane that seemed to go on forever, with a windbreak of black pine trees on one side and a pasture full of curious cows on the other. At the end was a large old farmhouse, built right against a steep hill.

"It looks as though the hill would come right down on the house," Margaret said.

"It can't," Dr. Evans said. "It's solid rock. Wait till you see the kitchen."

He got out and opened the gate, got back in the car and drove through, and then jumped out and shut the gate behind them. Around the side of the house, in a snapping, snarling surge, came two tough yellow and white dogs. Dr. Evans ignored them. He got back in the car and slammed the door, and the dogs jumped against it.

"These people are old friends of ours," he said to Margaret. "They haven't seen you since you were a baby, so it'll be all right for you to come in."

He parked the car in the barnyard and reached into the back seat for his bag. The dogs raced around the car and jumped against Margaret's door. She began to roll up the window, as two mouths full of teeth came within inches of her head.

"Dad, those dogs — " she said.

"What? You're afraid of the dogs?" Dr. Evans seemed surprised. "They're just farm dogs. They're supposed to make a fuss. Here, you carry my other bag. They'll think you're a doctor. Dogs never bite a doctor."

Margaret took the bag in a firm grip and slowly opened the door. The dogs backed up and waited, growling so deep in their chests it was almost purring. She followed her father up the path to the door and the dogs came leaping after her, circling around, snapping at her feet. The skin on her back crawled with goose bumps. She held the bag so tight her hand ached. If I'm going to be a doctor, she kept thinking, I'll have to face worse things than this.

They crossed the narrow back porch. The screen door opened, and an enormous woman in a house dress and apron stood there.

"Hello, Doc," she said, "glad to see you. Harry's right here. Seems a little better. Doesn't pain him much today, he says. Who's this? Don't tell me this is Margaret! Harry," she called into the house, "look who's here!" To Margaret she said, "Why, you were in your buggy the last time I saw you."

They went into the kitchen. The screen door slammed behind them, and the dogs were left outside. They were quiet immediately, having done their duty. Margaret looked with interest at the woman, who was so swathed with rolls and lumps of fat that it hardly seemed possible. Some of the rolls were so large and loose looking that they were like pillows tied on. Dad ought to do something about that, Margaret thought, operate or something. Her flesh was like bread dough when it's ready to bake, shiny and bubbly. If you push it with your finger and the dent stays, then it's risen enough, and you can put it in the oven. But the woman had a beautiful, fresh-colored face, very pink over the cheekbones, and a lot of shiny, curly gray hair piled on top of her head.

Her husband, Harry, a wiry, red-faced man, was sitting in an armchair by the stove with his foot up on a pile of pillows. When Margaret saw the foot she forgot all about the fat woman and moved toward it to get a better look.

Harry's foot was swollen and lumpy and looked as sore as a boil, but the most interesting thing about it was the color. It was a dull purplish-red all over, shading here and there into blue and purplish-black. The color ended abruptly in a sort of ridge at the ankle, and the skin above that seemed unnaturally white and smooth.

"Well, young lady," Harry said, "what do you think? Ever seen anything like that before?"

"No, I never have," Margaret said. "Gosh, that's terrific. Does it hurt much?"

"Margaret!" Dr. Evans said sharply. "That's enough! Mame, show Margaret your cold room, will you, and let me talk to Harry, eh?"

"Come on, Margaret," Mame said. "My, I'm glad to see you. How's your Ma? You're not much like her, are you? And you don't have black hair like your Dad, either, but you're dark like him, aren't you? I guess, between the red hair and the black, you're just in between. Never mind, brown hair is pretty, too. Did you ever hear the song about the nut-brown maid?"

"My goodness, is that what I am?" Margaret asked. "A nut-brown maid?"

"Well, compared to all the blond Norwegians around these parts, you're pretty brown," Mame said. "You and your Dad stand out, if you see what I mean. Now, here's my cold room."

She opened the door at the back of the kitchen and they stepped into a cave!

"See? Goes right into the side of the hill. Wait, I'll light the candle so you can see better."

Inside, there were shelves built against the rock walls, lined with jars of jelly and canned fruits and vegetables, and on the floor there were bins of fresh vegetables, almost empty. On a great oak table stood two big pans of milk.

Way in the back of the cave, coming through a crack in the rock, was a trickle of water. It fell into a stone basin.

"Why, there's a spring!" Margaret said.

"That's right, as cold as ice. It falls into that hollow in the rock and then it must run away underground."

"It's beautiful," Margaret said, "and this is a beautiful place. I can't imagine living in a house with a cave."

"When Harry's grandparents homesteaded this land they lived in this cave," Mame said, "and then they built the house onto it, a piece at a time. See here, let me show you."

Mame stepped back into the kitchen and pointed to a spot halfway up the far wall. "There's Harry's grandma's spinning wheel that she brought from the Old Country, and her loom, too."

There was a wide shelf, perhaps three feet deep, which ran the whole width of the kitchen and evidently served as a storeroom. On it were a couple of washtubs, a copper boiler, an extra chair, and the spinning wheel and loom.

"I can't spin myself," Mame said, "but I like to have it anyway. I think it looks kind of nice up there."

"I think so, too," Margaret said. "You're lucky to have such a nice house." She turned right around, looking at everything in the room: the kitchen cabinet with the flour sifter, the blue painted cupboard full of yellow dishes, the kerosene lamps in brackets on the wall, the wood stove, the painted bride's chest in the alcove, the carved maple armchair by the stove.

"That's what that girl said," Mame said. "What was her name again, Harry?"

"Victoria," Harry said.

"Yes, I didn't catch her last name," Mame went on. "She came by here early yesterday morning and helped me with the chores. The hired man was away and I was late with the milking and she came in the barn and said could she help. Said she'd always wanted to milk a cow. Of course she wasn't much good at milking, though she tried, but she fed the chickens and fixed breakfast. She liked the house, too. Do you know who she is, Doc? Kind of peaked looking with long black hair in braids — old-fashioned, kind of."

"If you mean the girl I think you mean," Dr. Evans said, "no one knows who she is. She turns up in town now and then, and then she disappears suddenly."

"She's a funny little thing," Harry said. "Tom — you know our boy, Doc — stopped by at breakfast time on his way to work. He was going to put a roof on a barn over in

Pleasant Valley. This Victoria went with him. Said she'd always wanted to sit up on the ridgepole of a barn. A steeple would be better, she said, but a barn would do fine."

"Do you suppose she really got up on the barn roof?" Margaret asked.

"Sure. Tom stopped back later and told us. Said she nailed shingles all day and then disappeared."

"How old do you think she is?" Dr. Evans asked.

"Oh, about sixteen, wouldn't you say, Mame?"

"Oh, she can't be sixteen," Margaret said. "I thought she was about my age. Does she live around here, do you think?"

"I never saw her before," Mame said.

"Well, we've got to be off," Dr. Evans said. "I'll be back in a couple of days. Don't forget your bag, Margaret."

"I'll come open the gate," Mame said, "and keep the dogs quiet. Did they scare you, Margaret?"

"Sure," Margaret said, "I was scared to death. That's why Dad gave me the bag. He said dogs never bite the doctor."

"Maybe that's right," Mame said. "Your Pa goes everywhere and nothing ever happens to him."

The car was like a furnace. Dr. Evans's white linen suit was badly wrinkled, and his face shone with perspiration.

"At least we don't have to stand out in the field and hoe potatoes," he said. "I don't dare go very fast on this road, so we'll hardly be able to get up a breeze." But, of course, it was cooler the minute the car got moving.

"We're going to Jed Erickson's next," Dr. Evans said. "His boy is sick. You'd better stay in the car."

When they got to the Ericksons' Margaret was glad to stay in the car. The Ericksons had a bull in their front yard! He swung his head crazily from side to side and rolled his bloodshot eyes, exactly the way he was supposed to do. Dr. Evans walked right past him and disappeared into the house.

A few minutes later he stuck his head out of the back door and called, "Margaret! Bring my other bag!"

I can't do it, she thought. I can't go by that beast. She picked up the bag and opened the car door. I can't do it, I can't do it. But she was doing it. She walked very deliberately (don't panic, don't run!), with the muscles of her back pulled in so tightly that she felt like a hoop. He's *looking* at my back. He's making up his stupid mind. Someone had told her that you can always dodge a bull, because they're so clumsy. But I'm clumsy, too, thought Margaret. I'm so stiff with fear I feel like I'm made out of Tinker Toys. She looked over her shoulder. He was pawing the ground, getting ready. She ran.

Someone opened the door of the house and she ran straight in.

"Thank you," Dr. Evans said. "Now, sit down over there in the corner and keep quiet." He took the bag and disappeared into another room. Margaret sat in the corner of the sunny kitchen and waited.

When Dr. Evans came back into the kitchen, Mrs. Erickson was with him, and she looked scared.

"I'll be back tomorrow," Dr. Evans said. "We won't get these test results for three or four days, but the treatment's the same anyway. Try to get some rest yourself. Can you get some help?"

"My sister can come," Mrs. Erickson said.

"All right, call me if his fever goes up," Dr. Evans said. "Come on, Margaret."

He walked so fast she could hardly keep up with him, and she kept dodging around trying to keep on his far side, away from the bull.

"What's the matter with you, jumping around like that?" Dr. Evans said. He opened the car door and Margaret shot past him onto the seat.

"The bull, Dad!" she said.

"Oh, that," he said vaguely. He turned the car around rapidly and drove out of the yard.

"Is it bad?" Margaret asked.

"Is what bad? That boy? I'm not sure. Anyway I wouldn't tell you if I knew."

She tried again.

"My, that was an awful looking foot!"

"You should have seen it last week," he said.

"Gosh, Dad, you've seen everything, haven't you? And you're not afraid of anything."

"Are you trying to cheer me up, Margaret?" Dr. Evans asked. "Be quiet and let me think about this case."

"Okay."

Margaret leaned back and thought about the kitchen with a cave and a spinning wheel and how she had walked in front of a bull. And Victoria! They said she'd milked a cow and sat on top of a barn because she'd always wanted to.

"I haven't seen Victoria since Decoration Day," she said thoughtfully. "That's three weeks."

But Dr. Evans was not listening. His mind was back at the farmhouse, with the sick boy he had just seen.

"I hope to God that isn't typhoid fever," he said.

8

"WELL, how's Miss Godfrey?" Mrs. Evans asked her husband as she poured the breakfast coffee, "or does professional etiquette prohibit your giving your wife any news? Of course, I can always ask the neighbors; they'll know."

"I don't mind telling you," Dr. Evans said, "but little pitchers — "

"Margaret's not down yet."

"Are you sure? Well, she's getting over that paralysis pretty well. She takes a few steps and gets around in a wheelchair. But she has spells that leave her only partly conscious. She sleeps half the time, and one foot is as cold as ice. Her arteries just aren't much good."

"Can't you do something?"

"I'm doing everything I can," Dr. Evans said morosely. "Everyone dies eventually. I can't keep them all alive."

Margaret, pausing on the stairs to listen, thought, poor Dad! and, of course, poor Miss Godfrey too. She waited. Now they were talking about her.

"I really don't think you should encourage her," Mrs.

Evans was saying. "You don't really want her to be a doctor, do you?"

"If she wants to, why not?" Dr. Evans said. "Don't you think women can be good doctors?"

"Why, of course," said Mrs. Evans, "it's just that I think the way the world is, most women are happier in their own homes."

"Even women doctors have homes," Dr. Evans said. "They buy dishes and sheets just like everyone else. They have husbands and children, too. It's a great waste, making women do housework. Look at you."

"Me?"

"Yes," he went on, "you've got a degree in mathematics."

"But I couldn't use it here," Mrs. Evans said.

"I know it," Dr. Evans said, "and I'm glad you can't in a way, because I like to have you here when I get home. I just said it was a waste, that's all."

"My goodness," Mrs. Evans said, "I didn't know you felt like that. I suppose you think someone like — well — Milly Nelson should be a research chemist."

"It wouldn't be a bad idea," Dr. Evans said. "Anyone with as much curiosity as that old gossip has would make a good research man. In fact, if she were trying to find out what was going on in the atom instead of what is going on in town it would be a blessing to us all." He pushed back his chair. "I have to go now. I'm taking the fan."

"Who is the fan for, Dad?" Margaret asked, coming into the kitchen. "The Erickson boy?"

"No, they don't have electricity out where the Ericksons live," said Dr. Evans. "It's none of your business who it's for, but it's someone who needs it worse than we do." He picked up the fan and was gone.

"What are you going to do today?" Mrs. Evans asked.

"Nothing," Margaret said. "It's too hot. I'm going to lie on my bed and read."

"Tomorrow I'm going to be making jam all day," Mrs. Evans said, "and you'll have to help me. I want to get that fruit out of the way before we go away. So make the most of today!"

The telephone rang and it was Polly wanting to play tennis. Margaret said it was too hot, but Polly said running around would create a breeze so they would be cooler, if anything, and anyway, today the courts wouldn't be full of big boys.

"I'm going to play tennis," Margaret told her mother. "If Victoria should turn up, don't let her disappear again."

"Don't worry," Mrs. Evans said. "I'm as curious about her as you are."

When Polly and Margaret got to the tennis courts, Victoria was there, sitting cross-legged on the ground with her lap full of tennis balls.

"Look what I've got," Victoria called. "I've been combing the bushes for hours and I've found all these old balls. They don't bounce very well but they're better than nothing."

"We always use old balls," Polly said. "I've never even had a new ball. Aren't you hot in those clothes?"

"Terrible," Victoria said. She still wore her plaid skirt and boots and, as usual, she had on stockings, which must have felt like sandpaper. Her jacket and cap were gone, but she was wearing a long-sleeved white blouse.

"Listen, Victoria," Polly said, "I have to ask you before I forget or you run away, what's your last name?"

"I'm not going to tell you," Victoria said.

"Why not? You know who we are and where we live and who our folks are, and we don't know anything about you."

"Why should you?" Victoria asked. "Why should you know anything about me? What difference does it make?"

"But it seems so funny — " Margaret said.

"Why?"

"Oh, forget it, then," Polly said. "You certainly don't have to tell us anything you don't want to."

"That's right, I don't," Victoria said. She began to toss the tennis balls up and catch them.

"Oh, come on, let's play tennis," Margaret said.

"Do you know I've never played tennis in my whole life?" Victoria said.

"I suppose that's another thing you've always wanted to do, like roofing a barn and milking a cow?" Margaret asked.

"How did you know about that?" Victoria asked. "I *would* like to play tennis, but I don't know how. You two play first and show me."

So Polly and Margaret raced back and forth on the court and wore themselves out, and then they took turns playing more slowly with Victoria.

"When that shadow," Victoria said, pointing to the shadow cast by the net post, "gets to there, I have to go." And she did. "Just like the Red Queen," Polly said afterward, "she went so quickly."

As Polly and Margaret watched her run across the play-field, the same thought came to them at the same time.

88

They turned to each other and said, almost at once, "Let's follow her."

Quickly, they stowed the rackets and balls in a hollow at the back of the court and set out after Victoria.

"Walk slowly until she gets beyond the house up there," Polly said.

"If we went through backyards while she's on the sidewalk, we could run without her seeing us," Margaret said.

"We can't just walk behind her, that's for sure," said Polly.

"She can't run forever. She'll have to walk sometimes and then we can catch up."

Victoria went straight out of town. She didn't run all the time, and the girls, dodging from house to house, kept her in sight easily. Once out of town, she set off across the fields, climbing fences, jumping ditches, walking between rows of corn, around the grainfields, and across pastures. It was hard for Polly and Margaret to keep under any sort of cover in this open country, and their route, which involved stopping behind fences and sprinting to the next fence corner or stand of trees, was roundabout and exhausting. Bushes and barbed wire scratched them, the sun beat down on them, dust from dry fields choked them, and mosquitoes bit them.

"I've never been so hot in my entire life," Polly said, "but it's worth it to find out where she's going."

"Why do you suppose she wouldn't tell us?" Margaret asked.

"Well, it isn't any of our business, I suppose," Polly said. "Maybe she lives in a hobo camp or something, and she's ashamed."

"Why should she be? We wouldn't care," Margaret said. "Anyway, I think hobo camps are just for men."

"Maybe she thinks we'd mind," Polly said. They walked through a creek, and for a while their wet tennis shoes felt cooler. Then they began to dry and it was like walking on sandburrs.

"Look where she's going now," Polly said, "right toward the river."

"There's nothing down there but swamp."

The river made a bend just where they were. The land enclosed in the bend was low-lying and marshy. The grass grew in hummocks, and when you stepped on it water oozed up. The girls saw Victoria leaping from hummock to hummock.

"There's no place for her to go," Polly said, "unless she has a boat. Anyway, if we go out on that marsh she'll see us." They stayed crouched behind a willow tree.

"We'll just wait," Polly said. "She'll have to come back and then we'll go on following her."

"I'm so tired," Margaret said. "I'm just going to rest while I can."

"So am I," Polly said. They leaned their heads on the willow trunk and closed their eyes.

When they opened them, Victoria was across the river!

"How did she get there? She couldn't have swum that fast. And I don't see any boat."

"We can't go any farther. She's beaten us."

Again, the girls peered around the willow tree at Victoria. She turned around and looked straight toward them. Then she thumbed her nose!

"She must have seen us!"

"She couldn't have. We're too far away."

"Then she just knew we were there."

Victoria walked on and disappeared among the trees on the opposite bank.

"Well, we might as well go home," Polly said.

"Do you feel silly?" Margaret asked.

"Quite a bit."

They walked slowly back across the fields, under the broiling sun.

"You know," Polly said, "that was kind of fun."

"That's what I was thinking," Margaret said. "Dodging and running and keeping out of sight — we'd probably get pretty good at it if we practiced."

"I can think of lots of people to spy on, too," Polly said carelessly.

"So can I," Margaret said. "Of course it's a little dishonorable. Emilie probably wouldn't do it."

"We could do it for some good cause," Polly said.

"Like what?"

"Oh, righting wrongs somehow," Polly said vaguely. "I can't think of any now but we'll probably think of new things as we go along."

"Tomorrow," Margaret said, "my mother and I have to make jam all day, because one of Dad's patients brought us a lot of some kind of fruit to pay a bill, and the next day we're going to Grandma's. We'll be gone two weeks."

"Belle will probably help me follow Victoria if we get a chance while you're gone," Polly said, "and I'll probably think of some spying jobs, too."

"I can hardly wait to get back," Margaret said.

9

MARGARET had a wonderful time at her grand-mother's, and she came back fully expecting to brag about her adventures there to her stay-at-home friends, but, as it turned out, so much had happened while she'd been away that she was the one who did the listening.

They'd had a cyclone and she'd missed it!

Margaret's father took Margaret and her mother out to see a road where the cyclone had chopped off all the trees. They were all half as high as they used to be and looked like telephone poles.

"It came right over the Lutheran church," Belle said, "and it looked exactly like the pictures, just a big gray funnel. We thought sure the church was going to collapse, but it lifted up a little and went out into the country."

"Did you stand there and watch it?"

"You might as well," Belle said. "If it's going to get you it's going to get you. There's no place to hide. If you run inside a building, something may fall on you. Look at Lenny Marston."

Lenny Marston had been killed during the storm, hit by a falling beam when a shed collapsed.

"It took a model-T Ford out of a barnyard, put it on top of a hill and turned its headlights on," Polly said.

"There was this farmer's wife," Emilie said, " — I've forgotten her name but Mama knows her. She was in the house with the baby when the cyclone hit and she was scared to death, so she took the baby and ran out to the barn to find her husband. Just as she got into the barn, the cyclone hit it, but luckily she was blown under the manure spreader or she would have been squashed."

"Squashed!" Margaret repeated. "What happened to her husband?"

"Oh, he was all right. He was looking for her outside somewhere."

But the shocking, the awful, the unbelievable thing was that Lenny Marston was dead.

They didn't mourn him as a friend, or even as an acquaintance of long standing. He and his family had been in town only a few months. He'd come to school the last few weeks, in May, but the girls had hardly known him. The first thing Margaret thought was, "But he was only as old as I am."

Of course, everyone knows children can die. Adults, indeed, were always warning them about crossing streets, swimming in the river, climbing sandstone cliffs, or lighting fires. Children *can* die, but whoever heard of one doing it? Old people, even middle-aged people died sometimes, and occasionally babies who were too young for anyone to know very well, anyway. But this had been someone their own age!

96

"He had a huge funeral," Polly said. "The whole town went. We went, because the Junior Choir sang."

"Did you cry?" Margaret asked.

"No, I didn't," Polly said. "I just felt sort of funny. But everyone else did. Every mother there simply sobbed, except Lenny's own mother didn't. Mama said she was cried out. I asked Daddy why people cried over someone they didn't know, and he said it brought eternity too close. It makes you realize how perilous life is, he said."

"I guess that's what's the matter with me," Margaret said. "I'm scared. When you think of all the things we've done — why, we could have been killed anytime!"

"Do you want to see his grave?" Polly said.

"Sure."

The four of them walked solemnly along the park road and climbed the steps to the cemetery gate. Lenny's grave was in the oldest, prettiest part of the cemetery, where the trees were tallest. Although the weather was dry and had been dry for weeks, the grass here was fresh and green.

"His family lived in town years ago," Belle said, "and this is a family plot. That's why he's in the old part."

There was no grass on Lenny's grave, but it had been planted over, solidly, like a blanket, with pansies. Only bits of raw earth showed.

"It's very pretty," Margaret said, "but it looks awfully short." She lay down on the grass beside the grave.

"It's longer than you are," Polly said.

"Get up, Margaret," Belle said. "You look ridiculous, lying there."

"Do you think, while we're here, that we should water

the pansies?" Emilie said. "It's so dry, and it never rains anymore. Papa says the crops are going to dry up and blow away."

"There's a faucet around here somewhere," Belle said.

They found the faucet and a watering can and watered the pansies, and then they walked aimlessly toward the other end of the cemetery, toward the country. In this part the trees were small, there was little shade, and the grass was yellow and so dry it was slippery. The sun shone pitilessly; it looked like a hunk of brass. In the fields beyond the cemetery the earth was cracked like a broken dish and the stunted crops were drying up.

"It does seem as though things are bad enough, with all the people out of work, without cyclones and a drought, too," Polly said gloomily.

"We're better off than they are in the Dakotas," Emilie said. All over the Great Plains the good topsoil was blowing away. The newspapers were full of it.

"Dad says Mother Nature is always ready to kick man when he's down," Margaret said.

"*My* father says *your* father is a terrible cynic," Polly said.

"I think we should think about something else," Belle said. "Ma says when you're feeling bad you should work real hard, but I think it would do just as well to play real hard."

"In this weather?" Polly said. "It would be cooler to sit down and mope."

"What could we do?" Emilie asked. "Of course we can climb up in Old Hickory and roll down the hills."

"Or we could coast down," said Polly. "I read a story in *Child Life* that said if you grease the runners on a sled you can coast on dry grass."

"Let's try," Belle said. "Your house is the closest, Margaret. Have you got two sleds?"

"Well, yes," Margaret said, "because Polly left hers there last winter. They're in the basement. Let's get them."

"And get some bacon grease or something."

Old Hickory was a piece of land too steep to farm and too eroded to grow grass for pasture. Consequently it was used only by children. For a couple of hours the girls dragged the sleds up the steep hillsides, greased the runners, and slid dangerously down, over and over again. Growing more daring as the time went on, they found steeper trails and higher jumps, so that they hurtled perilously down the track and flew through the air, riding their sleds like flying carpets.

"It's wonderful when you're airborne, but it hurts to land," Belle said.

"Especially when you hit a patch of dirt and go on your head," Emilie said.

"I can't do it again," Margaret said. "I've skinned both my knees and I'm worn out."

"Me too," Polly said. "What should we do now, besides rest?" They lay down on the side of the hill, in the poor shade of a bent oak.

"Does anyone know how Miss Godfrey is?" Margaret asked. "Dad didn't answer me when I asked him."

"Her landlady told Ma that she sleeps all the time and her foot is turning black," Belle said.

"How would the landlady know? Isn't Miss Godfrey in the hospital?"

"Yes, but her landlady visits her."

"Ma says she doesn't see how Miss Godfrey has lived this long," Belle said.

"What other news is there?" Polly asked lazily. "Have we told you everything, Margaret? What about Victoria? Has anyone seen her lately?"

"I saw her during the cyclone," Belle said. "She looked frightened."

"She looks different lately," Emilie said thoughtfully. "For one thing, she's so ragged. Her skirt is ripped around the bottom. And she's so thin, she looks half starved."

"She acts just the same as always," Polly said, "but, you know, a lot of people in town are getting worried. Nobody can find out anything about her. They think someone should do something about her."

"Like what?" Margaret asked.

"Well, if she doesn't have any family they think someone should take her in or she should be put in a Home or something."

"She wouldn't like that, would she?" Margaret said. "Does she know?"

"Ma said people have tried to talk to her and she just laughs and runs away," Belle said, "but I think she's keeping out of the way. She doesn't come to see us when there are any grown-ups around."

"I'd like to see her," Margaret said. "She makes me think of things I don't usually think of."

"Me too," Polly said.

"Like what?" Belle asked.

"Well, I can't think of an example. I just feel different."

"I wonder why," Emilie said. "She doesn't say much."

There was a long silence while the girls rested. Each was

sleepily getting ready to say "What should we do now?" when Polly said: "You know what. I've been working on a plan for scaring Martha." Martha was Polly's sister. "You know how superstitious she is. Well, I'm going to make a charm, and I need some small bones for it. Should we walk over to the horses' graveyard and dig them up?"

"I don't think horses have any small bones," Belle said lazily.

"Aren't there some pretty small ones fused into their hooves?" Emilie asked. "Seems to me we had it in science."

"Oh, pooh, science!" Polly said. "Everyone has small bones."

"I'd like to go," Margaret said. "I'd like to get a couple of bones myself."

"What for?" Belle asked.

"Oh, I don't know," Margaret said, "just to look at."

She didn't wish to tell her friends she wanted to be a doctor. They might tease her about it. She had an old anatomy book she'd found in the downstairs bookcase and she was longing to see the little holes in the bones that nerves and arteries came through.

"I think it's kind of dumb," Belle said, "but I'll come."

"So will I," Emilie said.

They walked over two hills, which would have been a short job for a flying crow but was a weary way to them.

The horses' graveyard was in a bit of wasteland at the foot of a hill, and whether it was a resting place for horses from just one farm or from many the girls neither knew nor cared. It was just part of their general knowledge that this was a place where you could find bones easily. The soil was loose and sandy, and either the graves were very shallow or the ground continually shifted, probably the latter, for the bones were close to the surface.

They scrabbled about a little in the warm sand and then pulled out a long skull and some ribs.

"Backbones would do for you, wouldn't they, Polly?" Emilie asked. "I think they're about as small as you're going to find. These must be backbones right here."

Margaret was looking over the skull. The holes were fascinating.

"What are you doing?" a voice came from above them.

They looked up, and there was Victoria, sitting on a rock.

"I've been watching you," she said. "I could hardly believe my eyes. What *are* you doing? Grave-robbing?"

"Just horses," Emilie said composedly. "It's not the same thing."

"Come down and dig," Polly said. "Why are you sitting up there?"

"I'm a disembodied spirit," Victoria said, "just up here sitting around."

She got off the rock and came down the hill. Margaret noticed that her skirt was ragged.

"You've been walking through bushes," Margaret said. "You ought to mend that skirt."

"This?" Victoria said. "It's just torn around the bottom. If I tore all the rips off I'd still have more skirt than you kids have."

"People are getting worried about you," Emilie said. "You should tell someone where you live and who your family are. Otherwise there's some people in town who are going to try to find out. They think you need more looking after."

"How silly!" Victoria said. "I live wherever I am. I'm living right here, right now. And I don't need any looking after. I look after myself. You can tell those busybodies so. The time is long past when anyone could help me."

"Now, what do you mean by that?" Belle asked.

"Nothing," said Victoria, and she got down on her hands and knees and began to dig too.

"Here's a nice, long, thin one," she said. She pulled out a slender bone, perfectly clean, with a slightly curved shaft. One end flared out like a table leg; the other end made a right angle and ended in a smooth ball.

"That's too small for a horse," Emilie said.

"Maybe it's a colt," Belle said.

"Or a deer," Polly said.

"Looks human," Margaret said, thinking of the picture in her book.

Victoria held the bone in her lap. She said thoughtfully, almost dreamily, "Do you know what I see? I see a little boy in a blue padded suit, flying a kite on a bare hillside. On top of the hill there is a — what is it? — a pagoda. There is a dragon painted on his kite."

"China?" Polly said. "What are you talking about?"

"Now he's a grown man," Victoria went on in her dreamy voice, "and he's on a ship. It's a sailing vessel. I hear the rigging creak, and the sails make a cracking noise in the wind."

The girls stared at her. They'd never heard her talk like that before.

"What's the *matter,* Victoria?" Emilie said anxiously.

"Nothing. Take the bone, Margaret. I've got to go."

"I'm too tired to follow her this time," Polly said.

"It's time for us all to go home," Belle said.

"I should have gone before this," Emilie said.

Polly took three backbones and Margaret took the skull and the bone Victoria had found. Belle and Emilie dragged the sleds.

"Let's hope we don't meet anyone," Belle said. "These sleds and bones look pretty funny."

Just below Old Hickory Emilie left them. Her house was just a field and a pasture away. The other girls plodded on, dragging the sleds. They were hot and streaked with dirt, and the bruises they'd gotten while coasting were aching.

"I wish I could go swimming," Belle said.

"We could spray each other with the hose," Margaret said. "It isn't far to my house now."

"But it's so dusty," Polly said. "By the time Belle and I get home we'll be dirty again."

Margaret got the bones up to her room and the sleds into the basement without anyone noticing. Then she ran the tub half full of cold water. They didn't have hot water in the summer. The water was simply too icy to get into. She went down to the kitchen and heated a teakettle of water and brought that up and poured it into the tub. That took the chill off and she was able to get in and get clean. By the time she was dressed her mother was home and supper was on the table.

"Well, where have you been?" Mrs. Evans asked. "I've hardly seen you all day. What have you been doing?"

"Oh nothing," Margaret said, "just — just trafficking with death."

"My goodness," Mrs. Evans said, "what does that mean?"

Dr. Evans looked up from his supper. How tired he looks,

Margaret thought, and sad and angry too. He must have had an awful day.

"Some days are like that," he said.

"What happened, Dad?" Margaret asked. "What did you do today?"

"If you really want to know," he said, "I cut off Miss Godfrey's leg."

"Cut off her leg!" Margaret said. "Why did you do that?"

"Because it was gangrenous," he said.

"Is she going to get better then?" Margaret asked.

"Not without a miracle," Dr. Evans said.

"That's enough, Margaret," Mrs. Evans said. "Don't ask any more questions. Just eat your supper."

Margaret looked over at Helen, who was sitting in her high chair eating raspberries. She wore only a diaper, and her hands and face and little round chest were covered with raspberry juice. Margaret looked back at her mother, who was wearing a housecoat.

"How come you're not dressed?" she asked. "What did you do today?"

"I got Helen all dressed up in her new dress with the embroidered panels," Mrs. Evans said, "and I put on my flowered chiffon, and we went to have tea in the Thorsons' garden. And Helen walked into their goldfish pool and I had to go in after her."

"What, that deep pool?" Dr. Evans said.

"It was over her head," Mrs. Evans said. "I was terrified for a minute."

"You mean she almost drowned?" Margaret said.

"I don't know about 'almost,'" she said, her voice shaking a little. "Anyway, she didn't."

We were all trafficking with death today, Margaret thought, only with me it was just secondhand.

After supper Margaret went up and got the bone Victoria had found. Dr. Evans was sitting on the front porch, smoking a cigar.

"Look at this, Dad," she said. "I found this in the horses' graveyard today."

Dr. Evans took it and looked it over.

"You found this *where?*"

"In the horses' graveyard."

"Whose land is that on?"

"Christiansons', I think."

"Well, I suppose I'd better call Ken Christianson," Dr. Evans said. "I had trouble enough today without this, Margaret. Why on earth can't you stay home and mind your own business?"

"I thought it looked human," Margaret said, "but nobody's missing, are they? Who could it be?"

"Whoever it is has been dead a good fifty years," Dr. Evans said, "so don't start speculating about it. Now, how am I going to tell Christianson that my daughter is a grave robber?"

He went off to telephone and came back to say that Mr. Christianson was coming right into town and that he was very angry.

Mr. Christianson was a short, square farmer with a square red face and round blue eyes behind round silver-rimmed glasses. When he arrived, he was so angry his bright blue eyes were almost shooting sparks.

"Is this the young lady?" he asked angrily, jerking his

head at Margaret. "Why were you trespassing on my land? What right have you to dig up my hillside?"

Oh dear, Margaret thought. "I — I'm sorry," she said.

"Now this," he swept on, pointing to the bone, "must have belonged to our Chinaman. Yes, that must be our Chinaman's thighbone, which, it seems to me, should have been allowed to rest in peace."

"But why was it in the horses' graveyard?" Dr. Evans said. "I'm sorry, Ken, but if I don't have an explanation I'll have to call the coroner, which would cause a lot of gossip."

"He wasn't buried with the horses, if that's what you mean," Mr. Christianson said furiously. "He was buried on the side of the hill, as he requested, but the soil shifts all the time — it's badly eroded — and I guess he moved."

"Who was he?" Dr. Evans asked.

"I don't know his name. It was in my grandfather's time when this Chinese gentleman came through Wisconsin on his way East. He was an old man, he got sick, and my grandfather took him in. When he realized he was dying, he said he didn't want to be buried in a Christian cemetery because he wasn't a Christian. He wanted to be buried on the side of a hill where his spirit could come out and look around. My grandfather, who believed in everyone being allowed to go his own way and do as he pleased, had hills aplenty on his land, and so he picked out a hillside where this man's Chinese spirit would have a good view of the terrain and buried him there."

"All right," Dr. Evans said, "that's fine. Here's your bone back. Margaret, if you repeat any of this, I'll skin you alive. Apologize to Mr. Christianson."

"I'm sorry," Margaret said again, and Mr. Christianson went off to his car with the thighbone of a Chinese upon his shoulder.

"Gosh," said Margaret, "I just wanted to study a bone."

"Stick to books," Dr. Evans advised curtly.

It was only later, when Margaret was getting ready for bed, that she remembered what Victoria had said, about the boy in the blue padded suit, flying a kite with a dragon on it, on a hill with a pagoda — how could Victoria have known the bone belonged to a Chinese man?

That's second sight, she thought. That's what it's called when you know things like that. If only Victoria would explain herself, but of course she never explained anything.

And what's more, I promised Dad not to tell anyone, so I can't even tell the girls that it really *was* a Chinese man buried on that hill!

Oh, I feel so terrible, so dumb and silly and guilty, she went on thinking. Why do I do stupid things like that? Dad looked really ashamed of me. He was so black looking today, anyway. Miss Godfrey must be going to die. I won't think about that. My baby sister could have been drowned. I won't think about that, either. I wish I could stop thinking I was lying on a bed of pansies.

Margaret went downstairs in her nightgown and found her father sitting on the porch in the dark.

"Dad," she said, "did it hurt Lenny Marston to die?"

Dr. Evans tilted his chair back and rolled his cigar in his fingers. "No," he said thoughtfully, "I don't believe it did. I was there, you know, when they got him out. We went at it very carefully, hoping he was still alive. When that beam came down and hit him on the head, he was knocked out. It wasn't like a chest or leg or abdominal injury, where he would have been in pain."

"You mean he died instantly?"

"Whether he did or not he wasn't conscious at the time. You were knocked out once, don't you remember, when you fell downstairs?"

"I was only out two or three minutes," Margaret said. "That was funny. I couldn't remember falling. The last thing I remember I was on the stairs."

"But if you'd been hit harder, and died," Dr. Evans said, "it would have been no different. You would have ceased to exist on the stairs."

"You mean I've died?" Margaret said.

"Essentially."

"And that's all it is?" she persisted.

"Well, if you had really died that time, you'd have lost your life. There's nothing worse than that. But the dying itself wouldn't have been bad."

Margaret heaved a deep sigh. This was a new idea. She didn't feel better yet, but she was going to.

"Dad," Margaret said, "is Miss Godfrey going to have a miracle?"

"No sign of it yet," he said, "but she's still going. Now, go to bed, Margaret, and don't come down again."

10

MARGARET woke early the following morning. It was light, but she knew it was early because it was almost cool and so still she could hear the milk wagon coming from a long way away. The horses' hooves clopped loudly in the early morning quiet, and the wheels creaked a little on the asphalt. Margaret got out of bed and knelt by the open window. The milk wagon got to their back door and the driver jumped out with his carrier of milk and ran up the walk. The horse walked slowly on, and Margaret saw a small figure drop from the back of the wagon and run, crouching, to hide in the shrubbery at the corner of the house.

Victoria!

Margaret hurried downstairs and out the back door onto the lawn. Victoria was behind the snowball bush, crouched down so that her plaid skirt was spread out on the grass.

"What — are you hiding?" Margaret asked.

"Just till the milk wagon is out of the way," Victoria said. "What are you doing out in your nightgown?"

"I saw you," Margaret said. "Listen, Victoria, how did you know that bone was Chinese?"

"I don't know," Victoria said. "I just knew."

"Then you shouldn't have given it to me," Margaret said. "You must have known it would make trouble."

"Yes," Victoria said, "it was just, well, just *mischief,* if you know what I mean. I was mad because Emilie was telling me I needed looking after."

"Emilie doesn't think that," Margaret said. "She was telling you other people think so, grown-ups. She was warning you. She said if you'd just tell everyone who you are and where you live then they would stop wanting to put you in a Home."

"I *can't* tell anyone where I live," Victoria said, "and I wouldn't if I could. Why should I? It's a free country, isn't it?"

"Not for children," Margaret said.

"Well, it doesn't matter," Victoria said, "because I'm going away. But I'm going to upset this town first. I'm going to turn this town inside out. Why, all I wanted was to do a few things in peace. There's nothing wrong with that, is there?"

"No," Margaret said, "and you certainly haven't done any harm."

"Of course not," Victoria said, "and do you know, Margaret, they're getting up a *committee* to decide what to do about me! The minister, and someone from the courthouse, and someone from county relief, and I don't know who else. Probably the sheriff."

"Oh no," Margaret said.

"Yes, they are," Victoria said. "Well, all I can say is, they'll have to catch me first. And they'll be sorry!"

"What are you going to do?" Margaret asked.

"I haven't decided yet," Victoria said, "but whatever it is, I better get started. That's why I caught a ride with the milk wagon, so I could get in town early and start fresh."

She started walking away and then she turned around.

"You can't imagine what it's like, Margaret," she said, "waking up from a long sleep, and being able to run free again and look at the world. That's all I wanted."

"I don't know what you're talking about," Margaret said. "Are you really going away?"

"Pretty soon. But I'll come and tell you good-bye."

Margaret watched Victoria walk up the street toward town. The amount of time I've spent watching her leave! she thought. More than I have talking to her.

The sun was coming up the sky. Its rays were growing stronger and hotter. The dew was drying, and the cool dawn breeze was giving way to the steady murmur of summer wind as it crossed and crossed the dry fields.

Margaret went back to her bed and lay there reading Book IV of *Bookhouse* until she heard her parents stirring. She waited until she smelled the coffee perking and then she sprang up and got dressed. One thing about summer was that dressing was easy. Underpants, dress, and sandals, and she was ready to face the day.

As she came downstairs she heard Mrs. Evans saying, ". . . and I got to asking around, asking people who've always lived here, who she was and where she came from. They said she'd come about twenty years ago. She was old *then*, really. She's worked in the library ever since. She's never had anything, just lived in that furnished room. If she had any good friends, no one knew it. Of course, no one was unkind to her, but no one paid any attention, either. I never talked to her myself except about the library. And now she's dying. I don't know, I think we might have been kinder, somehow."

"Well, you can't tell," Dr. Evans said, "she may have preferred to live that way. A very reserved woman, I would say."

Margaret had thought at first that they were talking about Victoria. Then she realized it was Miss Godfrey.

Breakfast was laid on the table on the back porch. Margaret went out there and sat down.

"Miss Godfrey didn't want anyone to be nice to her," Margaret said. "If she had she wouldn't have been so mean. I never saw her smile, not once, and you couldn't even touch a book not on your own grade shelf."

"Now, Margaret," Mrs. Evans said, "I did talk to her about that when you first complained about it, in the second or third grade. I didn't tell you what she said because I knew you d just start roaring around."

"Who, me?" Margaret asked, "roaring around? What do you mean? She wouldn't let us read any other books because she wanted to have her own way all the time and tell everyone else what to do."

"There you go, roaring around," Mrs. Evans said. "Stop talking and let me tell you what she said. She said it was just a small library, not like a big city library where you could pick and choose and still have plenty to read. By dividing it up into grade shelves she made sure that most of the kids would read every book, even the ones they didn't like at first try, and there'd always be new books to read the next fall."

"That sounds all right," Margaret said, "but I think that's just something she made up to tell parents."

"There's Lucy in my asparagus bed!" Dr. Evans shouted suddenly. He jumped up and went to the porch railing. "Hey, get out of there!" he shouted. The horse stopped stamping on the asparagus and looked up at Dr. Evans. Then she raked the bed a couple of times with her forefeet and cantered stiffly across the lawn.

"Dammit, I won't stand for this!" Dr. Evans said, and he went into the house.

"That horse! Why does she always pick on our asparagus bed?" Mrs. Evans said. "And I wonder how she got loose. Really, the Mosbys have been awfully good about keeping her shut up. I don't think she's been loose since spring, when she rolled on the first shoots."

Dr. Evans came back from the telephone.

"They're already out after her," he said, "Mosby and the oldest boy. They think Victoria let her loose."

"How silly," Mrs. Evans said, "why would she do that? By the way, I hear they're putting a committee together, to find out about Victoria. Do you know anything about that?"

"They asked me to be on it," Dr. Evans said. "I said I was too busy and anyway it's all foolishness. The child's been around since March. She's in good health. Someone's feeding her. Why worry? She probably just runs away from home now and then. She doesn't do any harm."

"But you must admit it's queer," Mrs. Evans said, "in a close community like this, where everyone knows everyone, for no one to know who she is."

"I don't see that," Dr. Evans said, "I meet new people all the time. Lots of people on the move. Lots of abandoned farms. People come through, live on one of them for a while, and move on. Now, I've got to get to the hospital."

But he was back in a minute.

"The side yard is full of chickens," he said. "I'm in a hurry. You'll have to do something about it." Then he hurried away again.

"Chickens!" Mrs. Evans said. "Whatever next!" She grabbed up a towel and hurried out into the yard. Margaret followed her, but at a distance. Margaret hated chickens.

"Shoo! Shoo!" Mrs. Evans was saying. "Run along home!" She flapped the towel and the chickens went running and hopping down the sidewalk.

Two Shetland ponies came down the street, stepping beautifully in unison as though harnessed together.

"Why, there are the Voldts' ponies!" Margaret said. The ponies broke into a gallop and entered the park road, shoulder to shoulder.

"My goodness," Mrs. Evans said, "I need some more coffee. Let's sit down and see what else goes by."

Margaret and Mrs. Evans sat on the porch and ate some more breakfast. They saw the Mosbys and the Voldt boy go by, carrying ropes. They saw a whole pack of dogs, some of them strange.

"But dogs are *always* shut up in the summer!" Mrs. Evans said.

"Listen to the birds, Mama," Margaret said. She'd been aware of it for some time, a persistent cheeping that got louder and louder until it hurt your ears. There were rabbits running in circles on the lawn, lots of them. All at once the air was filled with the chatter of squirrels. They almost drowned out the birds.

116

People came out of their doors, looked at the troops of animals that were gathering in their yards, and then went back in, looking a little frightened. No one was afraid of rabbits or squirrels or birds, of course, but in such quantity! Well, it made one cautious. Sooner or later, people could stand it no longer. They walked through the rabbits, squirrels, chickens, and birds and went over to their neighbors' houses to talk things over.

Margaret went in the house and called Polly.

"There are badgers coming up from the river," Polly told her, "and farm animals coming out of the fields. Have you seen Victoria? Everyone says she's the one that let the horses and dogs and chickens loose."

"Oh, pooh," Margaret said, "she can't be making the rabbits and squirrels and badgers gather around, can she?"

"Why don't you come over, Margaret?" Polly said. "We can walk around and see what's happening."

"Well, maybe," Margaret said. "You know how I am about chickens and birds."

"I'll keep them away from you," Polly said, "but I think we should be around because a lot of people are really mad at Victoria, and if they catch her there'll be trouble."

"Well, all right," Margaret said, "I'll tell Mama."

Out in the street in front of Margaret's house the mare Lucy was doing a sort of dance in front of Mr. Mosby. Mr. Mosby was hot and furious. The sweat was running down his face and he was cursing Lucy, who capered and shook her head like a colt. She's twenty years old, at least, Margaret marveled.

She went on down the sidewalk. Three crows appeared from nowhere and tumbled in the air right in front of her, cawing and reeling like drunken bums. Margaret got off the sidewalk and walked in the vacant lot. There were rabbits all over the place and they didn't even move out of the way, so she had to walk around them. When she got up to the church corner she went back on the sidewalk. The church steps were covered with dogs, sitting and lying about. She walked on and met a troop of squirrels, who were running along the sidewalk in a purposeful mass, tails waving, and scolding violently. She got off the sidewalk again.

She walked on up to Belle's. Belle and Polly were standing in Belle's yard.

"We just saw a muskrat," Belle said.

"The committee is meeting at the courthouse," Polly said, "and a lot of people are going up there."

"I wish we could find Victoria," Belle said. "I think she needs someone to stand by her. She can't be doing this, but everyone thinks she is."

"Look," Polly said. From where they stood they could see people gathering on Main Street. A herd of cows was coming up the street. They strolled along placidly, looking from side to side with kindly curiosity, like tourists.

"Let's *will* her to come," Polly said. "Let's all hold hands and wish at the same time for her to be here."

"That's dumb, Polly," Belle said, "but I'll try anything."

They held hands and closed their eyes. Victoria, Victoria, they said silently, come here, come here.

"I *am* here," they heard Victoria say, "but there's no need for wishing. I was coming anyway."

They opened their eyes, and there she was in front of them.

"Victoria, listen, the committee's meeting," Belle said.

"I know that," Victoria said, and tossed her head.

"We'll go with you," Polly said, "so you don't have to face them alone."

"I don't mind," Victoria said. "I'm not afraid."

"Are you really doing these things?" Margaret asked. "What things?"

"Letting the animals loose, and calling the wild animals."

"How could I?" Victoria said coldly. "I'm just a little girl, a little, weak, defenseless girl who has to be taken care of."

"Oh, stop it!" Belle said. "Don't be so dumb! You can't fight the whole world."

"Come and see," Victoria said, and she began to stroll up the street toward Main Street and the courthouse.

The air was now unbelievably hot and still. The wind had died and the heavy air pushed down on them. In this oppressive atmosphere the constant twitter of birds, chatter of squirrels, and mooing of cows grated on the nerves. Flocks of birds swept low over their heads. The sidewalk was full of small creatures.

"I'm getting scared," Margaret said.

"Me too," Polly said.

"Don't think about it," Belle said bravely. The girls grasped hands and, passing their bit of courage back and forth, followed Victoria up the street.

"The sun," Polly said, "it's gone. It's clouding over."

"Maybe it's going to storm," Belle said. "Maybe that's why everything is acting so funny."

There were a lot of people on the courthouse lawn. As Victoria approached they all turned and stared at her and a collective mutter, like thunder, passed over the crowd.

Mr. Mosby came panting up to her.

"Why did you let my horse out of the barn?" he demanded. "Don't deny it. I saw you."

"I'm not denying it," Victoria said gently.

"And my chickens," a woman screamed at Victoria, "my chickens are all over town."

Four people came down the courthouse steps. The crowd parted to let them through. They were the committee appointed to investigate Victoria.

The first to reach Victoria was the minister.

"My poor child," he said, "you must let us help you. You must have been very lonely."

Victoria stood perfectly still. The wind was stirring a little now, and it blew her ragged skirt about her legs. She looked very little and shabby.

"Not at all, sir," she said.

Belle, Polly, and Margaret came up behind her.

"She has friends," Belle said fiercely.

The Mosbys' old mare came walking down the lawn. She put her head on the minister's shoulder, snuffled loudly, and nudged him backward. Then she turned him around and shoved him out of the way so that she stood between him and Victoria. The minister shoved back at the horse. He swatted her huge rump with his hat. He grew red in the face. But the mare continued to push him back.

Miss Perry was the second member of the committee. She was a large, handsome woman with a high color, very commanding and firm. She always reminded Margaret of a big, red canna lily.

"Now, Victoria," she said, "we'll find a nice place for you

to live where they'll look after you and provide you with suitable clothes."

A crow came out of the sky and landed on Miss Perry's shoulder.

"What's the matter with my clothes?" Victoria asked.

"They're most unsuitable for a modern child," Miss Perry continued, rather flustered. The crow leaned forward and peered into Miss Perry's face. Another crow swooped down and sat on her other shoulder. He, too, peered into her face.

"Go away," Miss Perry shouted. She tossed her head and waved her arms.

"*I* think you're demented," Milly Nelson said to Victoria. She was the third member of the committee. "The things you've done. You should be shut up. If only Dr. Evans had seen fit to do his duty — "

Margaret thanked heaven mentally that her father was at the hospital where he belonged.

An old brindle bulldog, very rheumatic and wheezing loudly, came up behind Milly Nelson, and set his teeth in the back of her skirt. She leaned forward and screamed. With his powerful jaws clamped shut, the dog began to back up. Slowly he dragged Milly Nelson away.

Now the sheriff faced Victoria, as the fourth member of the committee. He was a kindly man and he looked embarrassed.

"I'm sorry," he said, "but you better come over to my office and answer a few questions. Can't have this, you know, upsetting the whole town — "

The wind now began to blow very hard. The sky became blacker suddenly and a sprinkle of hailstones, or pebbles,

fell on the courthouse yard. What with the wind and the noise the animals made, it was impossible for the watching crowd to hear what Victoria and the sheriff said, until at last Victoria said, in a high, piercing voice, louder than the wind, "You'll have to catch me first!"

There was the sound of galloping hooves on Main Street. The milk wagon, not built for speed, careened crazily from side to side in front of the crowd, pulled by a galloping horse. Victoria sprang away from the sheriff. She ran like a hunted fox through the crowd and leaped onto the milk wagon. The reins hung slack over the horse's back and draped down inside the cab. She snatched them up and slapped them on the horse's back. Then, sitting on top of the wagon, swaying and waving, Victoria disappeared from view as the horse galloped out of town.

The rain came down like a waterfall. The animals disappeared, and people ran home as fast as they could go.

Once it was all over, nobody quite believed it. Even Polly, Margaret, and Belle, safe and dry in the Johnsons' living room, hearing the wind beat against the house and the thunder rumble and crash, and watching the rain stream in sheets down the windows, could hardly believe it.

And they knew what Victoria could do. Other people in town really didn't. The girls knew that Victoria could see into eggs and stop the rain and cross the river without a boat. Margaret, at least, knew that she had second sight, and that she'd threatened to upset the town.

Mrs. Johnson rocked placidly in her rocking chair and mended a sock. "If you ask me," she said, "everyone's been pretty silly about this. It was just the dry weather and the storm coming, that's all that upset the animals. Anyone knows horses get wild when a storm is coming. My land, look at it come down! We needed the rain, but a cloudburst like this will just knock everything flat. And as for Victoria, the poor little thing was just having a little fun, that's all. She probably didn't tell who she was because her folks would find out she's been running away and traipsing into town."

(Polly's father, in fact, settled the whole thing: he owned the newspaper and wrote most of it. This gave him the last word in almost every crisis. People tended to believe what they read in the newspaper. When the next paper came out, there was a front page story under the headline ANIMALS DEMENTED BY DROUGHT AND COMING STORM ROAM TOWN.)

It was still raining when Margaret got home, but it had settled down to a comfortable patter that cleared the air and brought hope to embattled farmers.

"I've heard some of the strangest stories today," Dr. Evans said at supper. "If half of them are true, Victoria must be a witch at the very least. Or is it vampires that can command the animal kingdom?"

"If she really made that old milk horse gallop," Mrs. Evans said, "she can work miracles, and no mistake. You were there, Margaret. What really happened?"

"I don't know," Margaret said. "I can't remember."

She kept her eyes on her plate, but she could feel, through her skin, her parents exchanging looks and the unspoken communication: Margaret's upset; let's leave her alone.

Helen emptied her bowl of vegetable soup over the side of her high chair. "Raining," she said, smiling sweetly as she watched it fall.

"I got you some new books, Margaret," Mrs. Evans said.

"I borrowed them from Mrs. Hager. She has all Beatrice's old books. You better go to bed early. It will be a wonderful night to sleep."

Margaret took the books upstairs. She opened all the windows and got undressed and crawled into bed. New books and rain, what riches! Tomorrow the girls would get together and talk about Victoria. They would talk about her for days. But tomorrow would be time enough to begin.

She read one whole book and part of another before she fell asleep. The rain was still falling sweetly. It was a soaking rain, now, the kind the farmers like.

Hours later, she dreamed someone was calling her. She began to wake up. The rain was coming down with a rustling sound. She opened her eyes. The room was full of shadows, as usual, but there was so little wind, the shadows were still ones. Someone was calling her. Someone outside the window.

Margaret got out of bed and crossed the room. The street light lit the corner. The rain fell through the light onto the gleaming pavement. Someone was standing under the window in the shadow. A voice floated up to her.

"Margaret. I came to say good-bye."

"Victoria, you must be sopping. I'll come down and let you in."

"No, I haven't time. I brought you something. Can you open the screen? I'll throw it up." Victoria moved a little, out of the shadow. Margaret could see her clearly. She was wearing her brown jacket and her little plaid hat. Margaret unhooked the window screen and held it out of the way.

"What is it?" she asked.

"You'll see," Victoria said, and she laughed. She tossed something into the air. It flew up through the window, over

Margaret's shoulder, and landed behind her on the floor with a clatter.

"Good-bye, Margaret," Victoria called. "Don't worry about me. I've had a wonderful time."

"Won't I see you again?"

"No, never again. I have to go." She turned and ran across the lawn to the corner. There she stood for an instant under the streetlight, in the rain. She swung around and waved, and then she must have stepped out of the light, because Margaret couldn't see her anymore.

In the next room, the telephone began to ring.

"I'll be right there," she heard Dr. Evans say, and she heard him hurrying to get dressed.

He must have broken his own record, or maybe for once he had pulled on his trousers over his pajamas. She heard him run down the stairs, start the car in the driveway, and begin to back it out. Then she heard the car speed up the street toward the hospital driveway. She saw it pass under the streetlight, its headlights shining in the empty road, lighting the needles of rain.

Margaret turned on the light and stood blinking, looking around on the floor for whatever Victoria had thrown through the window. She found it under a chair. It was a little suede bag full of marbles.

She got into bed and emptied the marbles onto the blanket. They were her own, the ones Miss Godfrey had taken. She recognized every one. She held them up and looked into them. You can see things in them, she thought. You can see lots of things in them. But not an *explanation*.

Margaret sat there for a long time. She heard Dr. Evans's

car come back. She heard him come up the stairs, more slowly than usual, as if he were tired. He opened her door.

"What are you doing up?" he asked.

"I just woke up," she said. "What happened?"

"Miss Godfrey is dead," he said, and then he closed the door.

So now she would never know!

Dr. Evans was gone when Margaret came down the next morning, but Mrs. Evans was still sitting at the breakfast table, drinking coffee and waiting for Helen to wake up.

"Hi, Margaret," she said, "isn't it lovely and cool? The grass is greener already. There's french toast in the oven."

Margaret was half way through her breakfast before Mrs. Evans spoke again.

"You know Miss Godfrey died last night?"

Margaret nodded.

"She left a message for you," Mrs. Evans said, "Dad said to tell you."

"For me?" Margaret said. "She hardly knew me. And, anyway, she hates me."

"Nevertheless, she did. She said to look at the last book on the shelf."

"What?"

"Tell Margaret to look at the last book on the shelf, that's what she said," Mrs. Evans said. "What shelf, do you suppose?"

"Well, knowing Miss Godfrey," Margaret said, "she must have meant the fifth-grade shelf. I'm not allowed at the sixth-grade shelf until school starts."

"The library will be open in an hour," Mrs. Evans said.

The last book on the fifth-grade shelf was a volume of

the *Encyclopaedia Britannica,* the 1911 edition. That certainly didn't belong there. Miss Godfrey would never have stood for it. Margaret took the book and sat down at one of the tables. There was a marker in it, at page 14. The article on that page was entitled "Poltergeist." Margaret read all the way through it. The man who wrote the article seemed to be a staunch believer in supernatural phenomena. But what could you expect, for 1911? Two sentences, one in the body of the article and one at the end, were starred. Surely Miss Godfrey would never mark a book. Victoria must have done it, Margaret thought. The sentences were:

> The Highlanders attribute many poltergeist phenomena to *taradh,* an influence exerted unconsciously by unduly strong wishes on the part of a person at a distance.

> The Celtic hypothesis of *taradh,* exercised by "the spirit of the living," includes visual apparitions, and many a so-called "ghost" of the dead may be merely the *taradh* of a living person.

Margaret read this several times. She thought of things Victoria had said: "It's so nice to run again," and "You can't imagine what it's like, to be able to run free and look at the world again," and "There isn't enough time to do all the things you want to do."

Margaret got home in time for dinner.

"I got my marbles back," she said. "Victoria had them."

"How on earth did Victoria get them?" Mrs. Evans asked.

"I don't really know how she got them," Margaret said, "but apparently Victoria was Miss Godfrey's ghost, or spirit, or something. Did you know you can have a ghost when you're not dead? There's a Scotch word for it but I can't pronounce it. When Miss Godfrey started to black out or was unconscious, Victoria got loose. She was an astral body, sort of."

"Why, that's ridiculous," Mrs. Evans said, "that's the biggest mass of superstitious drivel I've ever heard. What's gotten into you? Why, I saw Victoria leading the parade myself! Everyone saw her."

"Well, the last book on the fifth-grade shelf was an encyclopedia, and it said it was an influence exerted by the strong wishes of a person at a distance. Miss Godfrey must have always wanted to lead a parade." Margaret turned to her father. "What do you think, Dad?"

"I have no evidence either way," Dr. Evans said, "except that Victoria had your marbles, but that doesn't seem conclusive."

"Do you think it's possible?"

"I don't think it's *impossible*," he said.

Oh, well, Margaret thought, I can tell the girls. They'll understand better.

Epilogue

———◆———

LATER, when the four of them sat under the trees in the park, Margaret did tell them, guessing, as she awkwardly tried to explain, that Polly, with her dreamy, wide-swinging mind, would understand, and that Belle and Emilie, who had their feet on the ground, would not. She was wrong. It was Polly who looked doubtful.

"I can see," Polly said, "that if you were old and stiff and you wished you were someone else, you'd imagine yourself as someone who could run. And her clothes were probably the kind Miss Godfrey wore when she was young. But Victoria was so real. She was realer than anyone."

"She wasn't, really," Emilie said, "because she didn't have any past. She didn't know how to go home, she told Margaret that."

"She was just invented," Belle said. "She ran around for a while and then Miss Godfrey woke up and she disappeared."

"You mean Victoria didn't know?"

"Miss Godfrey knew about Victoria but Victoria didn't

know about Miss Godfrey," Emilie said. "Why, Victoria was even afraid of Miss Godfrey."

"That was because she knew Miss Godfrey had the power to send her away," Margaret said slowly.

"But Victoria was doing what Miss Godfrey herself wanted to do," Polly said, "so she must have known."

"I don't think we can explain everything," Emilie said. "I don't think we can understand it at all. I don't know how much they knew about each other. All the book said was that Victoria was made of Miss Godfrey's unconscious wishes. That could mean anything. I mean, it's funny that we believe it, isn't it? But I do."

"I knew all the time," Belle said, "that is, I didn't really know, I just felt something. Because of the dog. That puppy George and Bobby were playing with was the *taradh* of the mangy old dog."

"Do you suppose," Polly said, "that when we're dying we'll get loose from our sad old bodies and do things we've always wanted to do?"

"I won't," Emilie said, "because I'm going to do everything before I get old."

"But we'll keep thinking of things," Polly said, "there'll never be an end to the things we want to do."

They saw themselves, the four of them, bent old crones walking down the street together, while up in the hills their *taradhs,* in washed-out, too-short summer dresses, were running races and leaping ditches. But it was a silly thought, really, because each one knew that she would never grow old.